DEATH PICKS A BLUE PALETTE

Also By William D. Skees

Computer Software for Data Communications
Before You Invest In A Small Business Computer
Writing Handbook for Computer Professionals
A Blush of Maidens, A Foolishness of Old Men
(WITH PETER J. FELL, M. D.)
The Doctor's Computer Handbook

Death Picks a Blue Palette

A Rayanne, Noor and Sandy Mystery

William D. Skees

Author of A Blush of Maidens,
A Foolishness of Old Men

iUniverse, Inc.
New York Lincoln Shanghai

Death Picks a Blue Palette

A Rayanne, Noor and Sandy Mystery

iUniverse books may be ordered through booksellers or by contacting:

iUniverse
2021 Pine Lake Road, Suite 100
Lincoln, NE 68512
www.iuniverse.com
1-800-Authors (1-800-288-4677)

ISBN-13: 978-0-595-43638-5 (pbk)
ISBN-13: 978-0-595-87963-2 (ebk)
ISBN-10: 0-595-43638-2 (pbk)
ISBN-10: 0-595-87963-2 (ebk)

Printed in the United States of America

CHAPTER 1

▼

A Most Unlikely
Detective

In the mirror one breast hung slightly lower than the other. Rayanne looked at it critically, working the tip of her tongue against her cheek. Definitely lower, she decided. On her easel she sketched in two perfectly matching breasts, nicely rounded and equidistant from the shoulders.

Rayanne took another critical look. One nipple seemed less perky than the other. She plucked her glasses off the easel and looked more closely into the mirror. Definitely less perky. She lightly penciled two equally perky nipples onto the canvas.

Rayanne squared her shoulders and stretched, basting her backside in the warmth of her portable heater. She took a guilty moment from her work to savor the heater's gentle magic working the backs of her thighs. She twisted to admire the lift of her buttocks in her reflection. This would be a good work.

The canvas on her easel showed light pencil strokes outlining the skylights soaring behind and above her, with bowed plank shelving spilling books and paints along the walls around her. The easel itself had been sketched in, with a faint image of herself frontal on it, and the mirror, full length, with tiny spider cracks, just beyond it. The central figure was herself turning toward an invisible viewer who had just interrupted her nude self portrait. A nod to the master painter, Velasquez, she had thought to herself when the idea came to her. But only a nod. This was going to be a "way different" painting.

The finished work would use lots of blue. This was a strong feeling she had already. Except maybe her hair. She hadn't decided about that. Rayanne's hair was auburn. All red, she was proud to claim. Perhaps too proud. Maybe where hair showed she'd use a blue that threatened to escape the mannerly family of blues, like ultramarine with its sense of floating in a bath of red.

She was not actually proud of her hair or her body, she told herself. She was just being candid. Candor was appropriate karma for an artist. An artist painting her masterpiece.

This self portrait could be her masterpiece and it would be titled, modestly, "A Study in Blue."

Modesty was also an appropriate virtue for an artist whose hardback retrospective *Rayanne Tellsworth—Cezannette* was even now, according to the publisher's graphic arts editor, on its way to the printers. And the best part of all was that it was going to be published anyway, even without her father's financial backing.

But, speaking of candor, that was what she was all about, she told herself again. And candor was the reason Señor Cee was on the canvas, too, preening himself in the shadows of one corner. Señor Cee was brindle, a tomcat whose lifted tail, like a shepherdess's crook, came just about to mid thigh when he curved his back around her legs as she painted.

This, the updraft from the heater, and the tender tickling of fine dust rising against her instep when she shifted her feet within the small circle she allowed herself were the three things she liked best about working this way.

That, and the complete freedom to move about, to admire herself, to reinvent herself, and to enjoy the delicate, whispering breezes of her own gestures.

That, and the north light that allowed her to feel golden in her skin, at least until she started to paint. That was when the dabs of blue would begin to appear, smearing her skin as she swiped at them.

She did not care for the feel of turpentine on her skin. She'd try to remember to get a tan this year. Auburns *could* tan. Thicker skin, that was all she needed. A thicker skin, the story of her life.

Her attention floated back to the thin strokes she had applied to her hipline and she looked critically at the shadowed dot of her belly button, double checking its position relative to the contours of her breasts and hips—vertically and horizontally.

The phone rang, loud and insistent.

"Damn," she said.

CHAPTER 2

▼

CLASS

"… otherwise you will be late again, and we will have to let you go." The words replayed in her mind as she bent slightly over the canvas to block out the wedge of her toes, proudly correcting for the Roman toe, big toe shorter than the second toe. The words "let you go" were like a cloud, a dark recollection of some nearly forgotten and unpleasant responsibility …

… unpleasant responsibility …

… responsibility …

"Shit! My class!"

She looked down at her watch, lying on its side on the table by her clothes, its dial face tilted toward her. The hands seemed awfully close together. She snatched up her glasses. Eleven o'clock. "Damn."

She grabbed an ankle length print dress off a chair, pulled it over her head, stuffed her hair down in the collar where the ends prickled lightly at her skin in front and behind, snatched up her sneakers, ran barefoot out the door, which slammed and locked behind her ("Oh, Christ!"), and started down the steps. The stairs were soft brown oak like her studio floor and felt comfortably dirty against the soles of her feet.

How does dusty-dark brown feel, she asked herself, pausing for a moment to brush her instep tentatively against the edge of the worn tread of the staircase. Shivers ran up the insides of her thighs … like this!

Her granny glasses were in the bodice pocket of her dress. She slid the wire ends through her hair with her free hand and hooked them over her rather small ears, flipped the ends of her hair out of the dress and forward over her shoulders and walked barefoot into the clump of students at the foot of the stairs, carrying her sneakers.

"Why are we all out in the hall?" she asked.

"Door's locked."

"Carlene's s'posed to open up. She here?" Rayanne looked around. Carlene was today's model.

Carlene was miscast as an artist's model, Rayanne had felt from the beginning, should have been a runway model, not an artist's model. Carlene was tall and thin. Magnificent cheek bones. High set ears, nearly pointed on top. Exotic. Definitely exotic. Carlene would have made a perfect runway model. She had the build for it, the walk for it, and the stamina for it. But, as an artist's model ... personality of a turnip.

Carlene had a dull way of looking at you when you spoke to her. Not so much as if your words were hard to understand. More like she had to keep recalling herself, bringing her attention back from her world to yours so she could focus on what you might have just said. To reflect on whether it was relevant to her personally. A perfect runway model.

Carlene, shit, where was she? This model was always on time, usually way early. Personality of a turnip, yes, but always on time.

Rayanne stretched up on tiptoe, still barefoot, and felt around with her fingers on top of the hall fire extinguisher while the little crowd watched. Then, key in hand, she opened the door.

Her students followed her into the studio carrying their personal wooden artists' boxes. They got busy collecting odds and ends from the studio room's various shelves and began to set up their easels.

"Everybody here?" She looked over her spectacles at the rickety easels being assembled in a half circle facing the tiny riser. "Six."

She sat on the riser and slipped on her sneakers. No laces. One tongue hung out sideways, the other slipped inside where it bunched up over her toes. It was her left foot, the smaller one. The crumpling felt ... not so much painful as ... interesting. She would have to remember to paint how a crumpled tongue felt against bare skin in a canvas sneaker.

She raised her chin till the familiar naughty-girl shiver ran up her back as she centered her vision on the rims of her glasses. Above them were the dark oaks in sharp focus, the pines of high ceilings and the upper walls of her small classroom-studio while, shimmering through the lenses, beginning just below glowing wire rims, stood the easels, the paints and carts. Underneath the easels lay the same soft wood floor that made her ache to slip off her sneakers and slide the soles of her feet lightly, ever so lightly, across the dusty boards, as if in a bath of talcum, till her nerves sang and orgasm loomed.

She shivered as she moved her shoulders and hips around inside her granny dress. Come back, Rayanne, she told herself. Back to reality.

She raised her eyes to the class. They were all taller than she was, the women as well as the men. Their easels were primed. Pencils on trays. Oils and turps at hand. Six students, a full class.

On Rayanne's left was an eighteen year-old art student from the Corcoran gallery's art school across the Potomac River in the District. Jasmine, who wanted to be called Jazz, had signed herself into Rayanne's class for the first time last semester. Actually she had begged Rayanne to take her. Her year at the Corcoran had been too demanding.

Jasmine wanted to paint, she had said, but what she had found herself doing was much too technical. She had fled to George Mason University up in nearby Fairfax county but had gotten turned off by the lecture format. "I just want to paint. That's all. I don't want to get tangled up in all of that other stuff." She would stick with Rayanne, she decided after her first semester in the Old Town Alexandria art school. "I'm learnin' by doin' or I'm dyin' a' tryin'." She rhymed when she could and rhythmed when she couldn't.

Two of the other women were housewives, as far as Rayanne knew. Ginger was just like her name, peppery and red. Madeline, who always came with Ginger, was dark-haired.

Ginger had a mass of curls, some usually dangling over her forehead. Rather than streak her skin with paint she'd blow at the stray curls by crinkling up the corner of her mouth and puffing through the tiny hole, her eyes raised askew. On the quietest of days, with everyone else working intently, there would come the sound, like gas escaping, of Maddie blowing at her curls.

Like Pop-eye the Sailor Man in mid-blow, Rayanne thought. All Ginger needed was a pipe.

The fourth woman was a government worker with her twenty years in, still young in her forties and searching for a larger meaning in life, for joy, for the sort of joy that only artistic fulfillment might bring. Eileen was petite and athletic, her calves a little too bulged from heavy lifting, hands a little too squared from too much chinning, face a little too rough from too much sun. A woman who needed less time in the gym and more time at her easel.

Mitchell and Philip were the only two men in the class. Both were government retirees. Mitchell had worked in the Justice Department. Philip had worked for the Navy as a civilian employee.

Mitch and Phil were of similar habits. Both men had trouble dressing casually, even for art class. Both men wore dress shirts, typically in pastels of light yellow or blue. Both men used aprons to protect flannel or twill in the winter. In summer it was khaki trousers. Both were graying. Both had short cut hair. Mitch's face was rounder, with full cheeks. Phil's face was lean with a long jaw and a British gunnery sergeant's moustache.

The first season in Rayanne's class Mitch had tried to grow a goatee but he shaved it off, he said, because of the Colonel Sanders jokes he got from his grandchildren.

Mitch's round face had a pinkish sun-starved look. Phil's face showed too much time spent with rod and reel in the bright sun, even in winter. He had the use of a sister's condo on the Indian River in Florida and slipped down there monthly all year round.

The students were getting restless, fiddling with sheets of drawing paper, readjusting their easels, and talking jerkily. Still no Carlene, "Damn."

"Bathroom's locked," one of the women called out.

"Shit, what else?" Rayanne muttered, teeth clenched. She pulled out the door key from the pocket of her dress, turned the lock and jerked open the door. The single room, a holdover from days when the building had been divided into yuppie apartment garrets, contained a toilet, a pedestal sink and a tub, the latter used now and again for washing out paintbrushes.

Today the tiny room was overwhelmed by the ugly thing that hung from the rafters. It was naked and purple.

Rayanne stopped, bewildered.

Behind her someone screamed.

CHAPTER 3

▼

COELHO

911 sent medics, but the police got there ahead of them. The officers, Muhammed and Briggs, called for a detective. Ten minutes later Detective Lieutenant Coelho showed up, driving a blue BMW Z3 with a brown convertible top which he parked on the sidewalk blocking the entrance door. He immediately ordered the bathroom yellow taped and the studio closed. "Who's in charge here?" he asked.

Rayanne felt very small. She wished she had her shoes on. "I guess ... me." The last word was lost in the back of her throat.

"Yeah," he said, looking past her, "O.K., somebody tell me who runs this place."

"That'd be the office over at the Art Center," she said a little louder, leaning forward.

He seemed to notice her for the first time. "Hey," he said, "you got any idea who's in charge here?"

The two of them stood looking at one another in a tight pocket of silence while around them voices echoed and clashed. Rayanne felt a tremble beginning in her knees and working up toward her stomach. Into their silence and through the noise behind them came a sudden clear voice.

"Did you see her neck?" A male voice, probably Phil's, "Must a been three feet long!"

*   *   *   *

Coelho had forbidden Rayanne's students to recover their art supplies or even their jackets, scarves or running shoes till after the Alexandria police photographers had come and gone. Even then they were denied access to the room. After taking ID's and calling in everyone's names, Officers Muhammed and Briggs took the call-backs, then continued to hang around, wandering mechanically but unproductively, it seemed to Rayanne, from the sidewalk to the entrance, up and down the studio stairs, and in and out of the bathroom.

After a while Officer Briggs made a coffee run to the deli around the corner on King Street. He had asked Rayanne and her students if they wanted something. Mitch and Phil had each asked for a cup, black.

Eileen said she'd appreciate a coke. Briggs said he was only doing coffee, but if she'd like a decaf he could handle that. "No thanks," said Eileen, hurt.

Ginger wondered out loud could they go home. Coelho frowned. He dialed up someone on his portable phone. "Coelho here. What you got on Kohlmeyer?"

Kohlmeyer, Rayanne had remembered for him, was Carlene's last name. She had been surprised that she could remember such a thing in her state of mind. Maybe she'd only seen it once, when she'd first interviewed Carlene. Maybe it was on the assignment list each time Carlene modeled for her. Really she didn't know how the name had surfaced for her, but it had been there when she had searched her memory for it.

"O.K. Four-thirty," he said into the phone. Then he tipped his chin at Rayanne. She went over. "Hey, uh, you, art teacher. I'm gonna have to talk to you. Go outside?"

For Coelho outside meant sitting on the hallway stairs between this floor and her living space with studio above. He asked her Carlene's age, his voice echoing down the stairway. Anybody could hear. She answered in a whisper.

Carlene's age? Twenty-four.

Was she sure about that? Yes, why?

Well he had just wondered how she could have been so sure about somebody else's age. How come she knew?

She didn't know why she knew, maybe something she had seen. Anyway, she just knew.

Where had Carlene lived?

Eleven-fifteen South St. Asaph.

Was she sure about that?

Yes.

Why?

Why what?

Why was she so sure?

Well, again she had just known. But a lot of them lived there.

"A lot a' who?"

"Our models. They live in kind of a group house. Most of 'em have modeled for me. I mean for the Art Center. One time or another."

"Yeah, but what makes you so sure about the exact house number?"

"Well, I used to live there," in a smaller, worried voice.

"No shit? Excuse me.... You was one of them models, too?"

"Yeah, sometimes." She wished the interrogation hadn't gone this way.

"No kidding?"

"Well, not full time. We all used to model for one another, when someone was working on something, like a body of work ..." She let her voice go fainter and hoped he'd lose interest.

"You living there when she was?" He nodded toward where Carlene's body had hung in the bathroom.

"Me? Umm, no!" she was surprised he'd asked. "I'm a lot older ... they're all way younger ... I mean there's at least ten or fifteen years between us."

He looked at her.

"I mean, all the guys, I mean the people living there when I was there. They're all gone ..."

That wasn't exactly what she meant. She meant they'd all gone legitimate.

It had been a good time, a carefree time, an open, friendly, warm kind of time. And a loving time. But it was true that all the people who'd lived there with her were gone.

And all of them—she believed she was the only exception—had left the world of making art, of being creative and letting creativity breathe inspiration into your body, wake you in the morning, pull you through the day and give restless sleep to your soul at night.

All the others were out in the business world somewhere right now. Some were somehow still in the arts, but vicariously, like in the publishing business or selling art books and supplies. Or maybe docents—artist auxiliaries. She was the only one still trying to survive as an artist. And even she would now rather teach than starve.

She still saw some of them now and again. It was not such a large community after all, those who had had some fleeting if peripheral communion with the

Washington D.C. world of art. The official arts establishment around D. C. amounted to scarcely more than the university art departments in the metropolitan area and a handful of art galleries. Even congress and the local papers—who enjoyed nothing more than name calling, blame throwing and scandalizing over the disposition of National Endowment for the Arts funds—had nothing more to squabble over than a few thousand dollars

If you left out the federal government's own art galleries, which were administered through the Smithsonian, the collective governments of the entire Washington Metropolitan Area, including the federal government, spent less on art than a good-sized city like Philadelphia or San Francisco, or Minneapolis, certainly way less than New York City.

Small wonder, with such a tiny pie to, if not exactly fight over, then at least aspire to a piece of, that one by one the friends she had known from colleges and art schools had all drifted away, seduced or engulfed by automobiles or TVs, by salaries or by clean sheets.

All gone, except for occasional invitations to parties, or reunions at bars and cookouts in the suburbs. Most of them she had painted, as most of them had painted her. Most of her paintings she had given to them over the years, usually as wedding presents or house warming gifts. But their faces and their forms were still in her mind.

Some, for the briefest of times, had bedded her as she had bedded others, but the closeness of the years together had been visible, she had hoped, in all the works she had created of her friends. And she knew Carlene's painting would have been the same, she would have ended up giving it to Carlene.

Except Carlene had not been an artist. Had never been interested, not the least bit, in painting. Rayanne thought about that.

*   *   *   *

Coelho had said something. He was looking at her.

"All right then, you guys can go," he called out, turning to the group huddled outside the studio. "Have I got everybody's address and phone number? Yeah, then, go on. Get outta here."

Jazz and Madeline started into the studio.

"Hey, you guys. That's closed off in there."

Officers Muhammed and Briggs handed out their clothing to them. None of their other personal gear was allowed out of the studio. Mitch and Phil took turns in Rayanne's bathroom upstairs. The women simply carried their stuff away.

Eileen shouldered her bundle and headed south along Union Street. The two men, with Ginger and Maddie, crossed Union toward the parking garage. Jazz came out last and walked quickly around the side of the building, toward the river.

Rayanne walked more slowly, heading north across King Street, and entered the large flamboyantly renovated World War II munitions building. Inside the building, in the wing housing the offices of the Art Center, she felt herself surprisingly cold and matter-of-fact as she summarized the doings of the Alexandria Police department for Dorothy Stubblefield at her large pine rolltop desk. Two Art Gallery volunteers in smocks sat at kneehole desks adjacent to Dorothy's and listened, shocked.

Dorothy Stubblefield was the founder and managing director of the Art Center. Some artists make art, some teach, some hang around art the way groupies hang around rock bands, and some organize. Dorothy was a born organizer.

Once she had pulled together her largely volunteer community of mostly amateur artists and cajoled the city fathers into a long term, low rate lease on the munitions building and its annex Dorothy gave up making any art herself and threw all of her considerable energies into running the Center. She had done an outstanding job.

Lots of artists and their studios now occupied assorted niches around the building. Some, like Rayanne, not only worked there but lived on the waterside campus as well.

Dorothy Stubblefield affected a faded blonde pageboy haircut that fitted her like a too-small wig. She was a large woman, too large nowadays to stand hours in front of an easel, arms too heavy to raise and wave in the air heaping paint onto canvas. These days she was more comfortable sitting at a desk, her bulk spilling over both sides of her swivel chair, typing on a keyboard and talking on the phone. She wore one of those hands-free phones that fastened to her ear like an ill-fitting hearing aid and dangled a cord across her sizable bosom, threatening to rip out her telephone deskset every time she turned around.

Dorothy wore loose fitting dresses in light colors with tiny flowers and she did not like hearing about problems, especially problems featuring death and the police.

She dropped her fleshy elbows onto the desk and buried her head in her hands. "Jesus," she said, "not now."

CHAPTER 4

▼

VERAJEAN

Around noon the next day, Rayanne gave the waiter her order and handed the menu across the tiny red-checkered tablecloth to the woman she had thought was her closest friend at the Art School. Without looking at the bill of fare Verajean Hollowell said to the waiter with the ring in his ear, "The same for me—crab cake sandwich with French fries. Cole slaw on the side."

Rayanne watched the boy walk away scribbling on his pad. His t-shirt read, "We serve crabs and nice people, too."

She liked the Fish Market at the corner of King and Union streets. It was convenient to the Art School. Best of all, except for a hole-in-the-wall way out in Fairfax County, they made the most delicious crab cakes in the whole Washington, D. C., area. In fact the best crab cakes outside of Annapolis. Like most Washingtonians she was always forgetting Baltimore. Washingtonians think there are only two cities on the east coast, Washington and New York. To them Baltimore is just a big small town.

On the way over from Verajean's studio in the Art School building Rayanne had told her about Carlene's death and about the arcane weirdnesses of police procedures. She had only just finished when they sat down to their first beers. Verajean always preferred one of the cocktail tables that was just barely big enough for two people, and jammed together on the minuscule second floor balcony outside overlooking King Street and the tourists walking by underneath them.

Their chairs were only a few feet above the heads of the fast moving crowds below but Rayanne and Verajean could lean their heads close enough together to talk without raising their voices. This always surprised Rayanne. Voices carry up from below, that's what one of her early boyfriends told her. He had conscientiously taken the high school physics class that she had skipped.

You can hear a voice from under you more easily than you can hear one from above you, he claimed. That was why he always hollered up to her window at night. Nights when he came around after her father's bedtime. She never told the boy about the low whisper she would always hear behind her as she slipped out, "Be home before midnight or your dad will start worrying."

Now, finishing their beers, Rayanne and Verajean should have been talking about photography. Unlike Rayanne, Verajean had actually attended an art institute, a real school where they awarded an actual Bachelor of Fine Arts degree.

Verajean started off in painting and drawing then switched to photography. For a photographer Verajean was oddly conservative behind the camera but in the darkroom she was a genius. There was no chemical or optical process you could imagine that Verajean hadn't already mastered.

Verajean didn't want to talk about photography today. Neither did she want to talk about the pointless tail-chasing shenanigans of the Art School's administrators or the after-hours dalliances of the artists who shared her darkroom or about Rayanne's problems.

"Rayanne," she said to the back of her friend's head. Rayanne had turned away to thank the waiter who delivered the crab cake platters, and now brought herself back to look into Verajean's eyes.

"Rayanne," Verajean repeated, "this is important …"

"What is?"

"Michael and I are getting a divorce."

This must be serious. Up to now Michael J. Hollowell had always been Mikey Joe, and his misadventures in the Public Defender's Office had always been shriekingly funny. Now, all of a sudden, Mikey Joe had become just Michael, like a faded name in an ancient high school yearbook.

"Well," Rayanne said, after a long minute of trying to think of something appropriate, "marriages are tough. Sometimes they work out and some times they don't."

No response from Verajean who seemed to be expecting something more helpful.

"Is it going really hard for you?" Rayanne volunteered, watching for a reaction. Nothing.

Rayanne tried again. "Did you feel something like this was coming?"

That must have been the right question to ask. Verajean had a way of talking in uneven bursts, as if inspired and regretful by turns.

"Michael's already moved out … He's going to be all right … We've been talking about this for a long time."

It was Rayanne's turn again. What was the right thing to say? "Did it hurt you very much?" she asked in a small voice, her forehead almost touching Verajean's.

"It wasn't so much Michael's fault. Yeah, I think he'd been looking around but I don't think he's seeing any one person right now."

A pause, then, "He didn't leave *me*. I left him."

"Oh, I'm sorry … Umm, those things happen. You know, I guess a person doesn't always find the right man the first time."

"Who's looking for a man?"

Rayanne raised her eyebrows and puckered her lips as if an answer were about to burst out of her, but no words came.

"I'm leaving Michael … for … another woman."

Oh gee, it was suddenly quiet up here on the little balcony. Very quiet.

"She's a Marine. A sergeant. Stationed at Quantico. This is her last tour before her twenty and she's out. She's very supportive of my art. I've started to paint again."

"What about your photography?" Rayanne like was a desperate swimmer, drowning in a swift current. She would grab at anything to stay afloat.

"That will be my day job. At least till I can afford to quit. Meanwhile I'll paint nights. Weekends."

Verajean stopped for a moment and looked at Rayanne intently, her eyes moving quizzically. "Rayanne, listen. Stubblefield is really pissed about this."

Verajean waited for a few seconds.

"Rayanne, I'm talking about Dorothy Stubblefield, the director of the Art Center."

"I know who you mean."

"She's talking about replacing me."

"She can't do that." Rayanne said, but without conviction. "She has no reason."

To herself Rayanne was thinking, surely not an issue with sexual orientation, not in this day and age?

"What about your family?" Rayanne tried another direction. She knew Verajean was a strong family person. Come to think about it, she was always hearing more about Verajean's parents than about Mikey Joe.

"They've met Sandra … Sandy. They like her pretty well. They're not happy about this but they're accepting it okay. They said we were lucky Michael and I never had children.

Rayanne was thinking maybe it would have been better if Michael and Verajean *had* had children, but she said, "I'd like to meet her too, sometime."

"I'll call you some afternoon when Sandy comes down to the studio to pick me up."

"O. K."

"That reminds me," Verajean added. "What are the police going to do about Carlene's suicide?"

"It wasn't suicide," Rayanne said. "It was murder."

CHAPTER 5

▼

A WEEK LATER

"The police have made what they call a tentative finding," Rayanne said to the students standing around her. She had decided that she owed it to them to tell them at least what she knew. This was against Coelho's orders, which made her feel both a little bit giddy and a little bit brave. She hoped that what she was telling them would satisfy at least some of their concerns.

"They're calling it an apparent suicide."

Her class continued to stare at her.

"But they're keeping the case open." She sounded like a bureaucrat, she thought, adopting Coelho-speak. What Coelho had actually said to her was that one thing bothered him, something he wanted resolved before he closed the case, and he was hoping evidence would turn up.

Rayanne had wondered at the time what kind of evidence could show up in a four-by-four bathroom with a locked door, a bathroom the police had been in and out of for a whole week and wouldn't let anybody use.

Strictly as an emergency measure she was now allowing her students to go up to her combination studio-and-apartment when they needed to, but she hated giving out her key. Her students seemed to sense the imposition, and went instead across the street when they could.

Yes, she wondered what evidence, if any, might show up. But one thing she knew. Coelho was bothered, but whatever it was that bothered Coelho made

Rayanne certain. If he wasn't sure it was suicide then she was darn sure it was murder.

He hadn't meant for her to find out about the puncture wounds. To him they were an unsolved puzzle. To her innermost self they meant somebody else killed Carlene. It simply could not be any other way.

She tightened up her voice, dropped the pitch a tad, and assumed an authoritative look. "Okay. Let's get to work."

$$* \quad * \quad * \quad *$$

"Today we have Elba. Hers is a different body type from Carlene's ..." Rayanne's voice choked on Carlene's name, "... last week."

Her mind filled with an all-too-vivid image of the girl dangling, her neck stretched beyond any natural length. The girl's head had been so purple it was almost black. Rayanne swallowed and forced a long slow breath.

"Carlene was ... skinnier, bonier," Rayanne continued. "All elbows, sharp hiplines, prominent cheekbones, knees, ribs showing. Strong shadow areas. Straight lines, angular shapes. Small bright highlights. Today's model is ... rounder. You'll have curves to work with. Smooth shadows, soft features. Oval and spherical shapes ..."

Rayanne waved limply at the empty riser in front of her and continued, "... when she gets here."

"Hey! Behind you."

Elba had entered, a little breathless from the stairs, and came out of the shadowed corner to the left of the easels. She was sandaled, wearing only a bathrobe with rips under the armpits and frayed sleeves.

"Sorry. West light," said Rayanne. "Always does that to me."

And then, "Well then, let's get to work."

She steered Elba toward a pile of furniture by the wall. "Let's set up something interesting here."

Between them Rayanne and Elba dragged an abbreviated chaise lounge over from the studio's haphazard collection of junk and up onto the riser. Rayanne stuffed a big pillow against the backrest of the chaise.

Elba stepped up on the riser, turned her back to the easels, slid off her robe and dropped it between the back of the chaise and the wall. She toed her slippers gently off her feet, nudged them around behind the riser, handed her water bottle to Rayanne, and sat down next to the pillow.

Rayanne lifted Elba's arm so that the elbow rested on the pillow and the hand fell curving over the armrest. She stooped and slid the model's feet slightly to the side so that her knees moved toward the pillow and so that the curve of her hips began to lift above her waist. Then she had Elba rest her head on the other arm where it draped over the pillow.

"How's that?"

"Fine," Elba told her.

"You going to be able to hold this?"

Elba tested her legs, sliding them left and right then back to the middle. She raised her head and lowered it, closing her eyes. "Okay."

Rayanne set Elba's water bottle on the floor below Elba's waist where the model could get to it with her free hand and without changing position too much.

Shuffling and scuffling sounded as easels were dragged around and turned so their canvasses would be in the light and the view would be clear. Mitchell, one of the retirees, picked up his easel and carried it around to the side opposite the windows. His would be an unusual angle, with the top of Elba's head toward him. Ginny, one of the housewives, pushed her easel down on its legs and scrunched into a chair for a lower perspective.

Rayanne turned to the class and, raising her voice, surprised herself to hear the tone rise too. "This is a long pose. If the only thing you get done today is the sketch don't worry about it. We have Elba for two more weeks. That will be plenty of time, even for you who are doing oils."

She walked around behind the easels. She shoved at one of the stools on top of which a container of paints was precariously balanced. "Move this stuff in front of your easels so I can have room to walk behind you."

More scuffling and shuffling noises.

"Ready, set, go."

They picked up brushes, pencils and chalks.

Rayanne heard a yelp.

She spun around.

"Elba!"

CHAPTER 6

▼

POSE

"Sorry. Sorry. Sorry," Elba wailed. "Fell asleep. Dreamed I was falling."

Elba lay in a heap on the riser where she had slid off the chaise. It took a while to get everyone settled down again.

✳   ✳   ✳   ✳

Rayanne watched the steady work of the sketching pencils lightly roughing in the reclining woman. It was interesting to walk around the semicircle, getting six different perspectives of the same model from six different points of view. Taken together it was like a three dimensional image rather than a two dimensional portrait, as if they were building one single sculpture together rather than making six individual paintings.

She wondered if there was a way she might paint an image with multiple views, sort of like a Picasso where you saw the front view and the side view all at the same time. She thought she might try that later, using her blue self portrait upstairs. Meanwhile she had given her class long enough to get something down on canvas. Time to check their work.

"Maybe a little higher, don't you think?" This to Madeline. Maddie had a stray curl that always dangled over her forehead and by the end of class would hang way down between her eyes. Her hair was mostly black with scattered single threads of gray. But the one particular curl that arrived each morning tucked up under a sweatband and left each afternoon drooped between her eyebrows—that particular curl—was shiny jet black, an anthracite letter J.

Maddie ducked down to peer at the model. Elba's right shoulder did seem higher than she had drawn. Maddie raised herself on tiptoe to look. Yep. She swiped a fine line a half inch or so above the one she'd just made and rubbed the old one out.

Rayanne moved quietly from easel to easel, stopping each time slightly to the side of and a little behind each student. When she spoke she tried to keep her voice low. Even so she would occasionally startle a student out of deep concentration. It always embarrassed them both.

That was a particular problem with one of the retirees. He was short, and heavy-armed with thick glasses, behind which his gray-green eyes were enormous. It always amazed her when he removed his spectacles how tiny his eyes really were. When the model took her first break he put away his brushes and pencils, set his canvas up on a shelf, stood his easel in the corner, tugged himself into his tight down vest and walked out the door. By the end of Elba's second break the only other man in the class was gone, too.

Not unusual. Both men were short on patience and both smoked. But they worked fast and they'd be finished as soon as the women were. Too bad they'd gone. Typically, they would set up their easels at the extremes of the semi-circles which meant they had the most interesting angles and Rayanne was intrigued by the way their foreshortening had begun to emerge on the canvas. Good detail men. The little things—toes, fingers, knuckles, nipples, ears, belly buttons—were already visible in their work.

Typically, too, the women's easels were bunched, and though one painter was sitting down—which gave her image a slightly lower perspective—their work did not show the wide divergences of the two men's.

"How you doing?" Rayanne asked Elba as the model began to re-arrange herself in the pose. She was going into her third session with this same pose. They had logged more than two hours so far.

"Okay," Elba grunted as she eased her left arm along the pillow top to stretch the muscles. "This arm has started going to sleep. Yeah, and this leg's trying to cramp up on me."

Elba slid her left leg forward just a bit to ease the strain, the one on which most of her weight was resting. "I'll be okay."

Rayanne gave her a sympathetic smile and, in a louder voice so that all could hear, said "Check your model. If something's not in the right place, tell her now."

A moment of silence as the four remaining women looked over their sketches and compared them to the placement of Elba's various parts.

"Arm's too high."

"Chin's wrong."

"Don't tell her something's wrong. Tell her how to fix it," Rayanne directed them.

"Yeah, raise your left arm … no make it come forward a little bit. Nope, too much. Now to the left. No, no, *your* right. About there. Yeah, I think, all right. That's good."

"Anybody else? If you can't say it, show her."

Someone else came up and fussed a bit, moving Elba's right arm, the one that had been draped along her hip line, and maybe adjusted something else. Later Rayanne could not remember who it was.

CHAPTER 7

▼

CRASH

The remaining members of Rayanne's class had settled back into their routine. They were working slower now, penciling in details, adjusting lines, stippling at shadows, trying not to get too much weight in the sketch where the lead might show through paint. The chaise creaked as Elba leaned forward just enough to pick up her water bottle and take a sip.

"Sorry, I'm so thirsty."

Probably no one but Rayanne heard her.

Elba settled back. "O.K.?" she asked, checking her position. "God. This water tastes awful."

This third session of the class was usually the hardest on all of them. Rayanne wandered out into the hall where there was a pay phone. She left her name on a boyfriend's answering machine and hung up. She leaned against the wall. From her position in the hall Rayanne watched her students through the door as the urge to stretch worked its way through the class.

For a while there was a general milling about as first one of the students then another came out, joined the group, grinned or wiped hands at the hall sink, and wandered back in. Probably with all the going and coming, and the general press of blue jeans, smocks and sweat in the narrow hall, at least one, maybe all of her students at one time or another, had been left alone in the studio with the model. Rayanne wished later she could remember whether someone had and, if so, who.

When finally all the students were out in the hall at the same time Rayanne thought she ought to tell Elba to take a break. She wondered why Elba hadn't just gotten up on her own. Maybe she'd fallen asleep. It could happen. Some models claimed they could sleep while they held a pose. Some said they meditated. Some listened to music in their heads. Whatever. It all amounted to the same thing. She would wake Elba up.

Rayanne led the little group back into the studio, women's light voices filling the air behind her. Elba was in pose, a still form. Elba jerked up her head at the noise they made trooping back into the studio, her eyes wide with surprise. She struggled to sit up but fell backward off the chaise, caught herself, then stumbled sideways as if one leg had been asleep. She staggered away from them, fear in her face.

All at once Elba was no longer a figure study. What had been a nude was now just a naked woman. Rounded curves were now skin, heavy skin that jostled and collided as she backed away. Sweat spotted her chest. Her belly jerked in ragged waves.

Rayanne felt a sharp pang of sympathy in her stomach. What was the matter with Elba? She would comfort Elba. Calm her. She stepped quickly to the chaise, caught her leg and lurched awkwardly around the right-hand side, hands outstretched toward the model. Regrettably.

As if a monster out of her nightmares were coming at Elba, she twisted away from Rayanne and threw herself at the window, hands out in front of her. There was a crash. The windowsill caught her knees and her upper body toppled forward—out the window. Rayanne's memory flashed on falling glass and buttocks, the soles of bare feet and toes. Forever at that moment, and forever.

Now Rayanne was at the window, arms up, protecting herself from the slivers of broken glass sticking out of the aged frame.

Students crowded behind her, looking over.

Three stories below them Elba sprawled—a naked woman no longer large, face down, neck crooked, one arm beneath her, spots of blood spreading over the concrete around her. Fragments of glass, pushed ahead of her in a sparkling wake, lay glinting in the sun. The beautifully rounded figure was now angular and flat. It would never have occurred to her to paint Elba that way. It did not occur to her now.

Horrid image. God!

Suddenly fragile, Rayanne was the smallest of the five women hurrying down the steps, cool air inside her dress billowing up from the pavement outdoors. At least the others were dressed for the street. She was not dressed—only her thin soled sneakers between her and the concrete, only the meager fabric of her shift between her body and the outdoors. If they needed her dress for a bandage she'd have nothing to cover her. Nothing.

She was the last down the steps. The students huddled around Elba's still form. Rayanne faintly heard or thought she heard Jasmine say "I know CPR. I can do it." As Rayanne dropped beside the still form someone said "I'm calling 911." Rayanne touched Elba's shoulders with fingers suddenly wet, tears falling close and spattering off her nose.

Somebody helped her. Together, with one holding Elba's head and neck so they could turn her, and later, with Jasmine blowing on Elba's mouth and pushing at her chest, Rayanne's whole world was the flattened, blood-streaked face on the ground, with its wild eyes and its blue-grey forehead. That and the wetness of her own tears and her hot cheeks.

She knew already that Elba was dead.

And she knew she would always see her like this.

*　　*　　*　　*

"I was thinking maybe we should call her family," Rayanne said in a small voice.

"Go ahead," said Dorothy without lifting her head. Rayanne was once again in Dorothy's office. No one was happy.

"Don't you have her records?"

"Shit," said Dorothy. She waved a pudgy hand toward the girl on her right. "Kerri Ellen, for God's sake, get Elba's file, will you?"

Kerri sat up straight, a puzzled look on her face, then shook her head slowly, dumbly from side to side.

"You know, Elba," said Dorothy irritably, "Elba, for God's sake. Elba ..."

Dorothy waved her hand in slow, jerky circles in front of her. "You know, Elba. Elba. Houston. Yeah, Elba Houston."

Kerri Ellen brightened up a little and swung around in her chair. There was a file cabinet between them and closer to Dorothy, but Dorothy sat at her desk, chin in her hands, staring gloomily past Rayanne.

"I'll copy out her parents' phone number for you," Kerri said.

"I thought one of you would call. You know. Somebody from the office."

"For God's sake, Rayanne," said Dorothy still staring off into her gloomy prospects. "It's not like she was a full time employee or something. We don't even have medical benefits for models or nothing like that. Jesus, I hope they don't expect us to pay for her funeral or something."

There was silence in the room. Kerri Ellen handed Rayanne a post-it note with a teenager's bad printing on it.

"Jesus," said Dorothy, raising her eyes to the ceiling. "Wonder if our insurance will pay for that window?" Calling back over her shoulder, "Mary Jean, can you get one of the volunteers over there to clean up that glass?"

"And everything else," she added.

"It's all taped up," said Rayanne in a small voice. No one was listening.

"They won't let you in," she added anyway.

But the other three women had huddled up—with quarrelsome voices it seemed to Rayanne—over who would go or whether they could get one of the guys from the Art Center public information desk downstairs.

She took her salmon-pink post-it page and turned to leave the sounds of their whining behind her.

"Another one. Another god-dammed suicide," she heard Dorothy say.

"Oh, no!" she said and turned back to stare at Dorothy. "They both were murdered. You didn't realize that?"

CHAPTER 8

▼

JASMINE

"Suicide. Murder. What the hell difference does it make?" Dorothy Stubblefield raised her head on her hands to look up at Rayanne standing on the other side of her desk.

"Have you got any idea how many people would just love to see this place shut down?" she went on. "There's at least three or four on the city council alone, just dying to kick us out of here and turn this place over to the developers. God!"

Dorothy rolled her eyes and grimaced, her eyes disappearing into the swollen flesh of her cheeks. She dropped her head again and ran her fat fingers through the short straight strands of her hair.

"Jesus."

*   *   *   *

The pay phones in the great hall downstairs where the public walked through were not private enough, Rayanne thought. She considered for a moment going back to her combination studio and apartment, but she wasn't yet ready to pass the sidewalk with its yellow tape and broken glass. Neither did she feel up to climbing the stairs past the yellow taped doorway. No, she would find a phone booth outside, maybe on the docks.

The rear of the Art Center, the side facing the Potomac, was its better side. The back doors of the building opened onto a broad dock where excursion boats and small motor yachts tied up. North along the river to the left were tourists' restaurants built out over the wharf, featuring bars tiered and cantilevered over the water. Downriver to the right was a yacht club which, due to Alexandria's generations-old renunciation of its seaport heritage, had less of a "yacht" flavor and more of a "club" flavor, having degenerated into just another high priced place to have an exclusive drink.

At this time of day, late afternoon, the dock immediately behind the Art Center was full of people. There were tourists and locals alike in summer uniform, tasteless shorts and tops of various types. There were young couples, mothers with strollers, and teenage girls in twos and threes. Not for the first time Rayanne wondered where the teenage boys were.

There were also runners and bikers in expensive Spandex tights, the runners with water bottles, the bikers holding their water bottles in one hand, pushing their bikes with the other—husbands and wives in matching Spandex colors. The summer haze was so thick in the heat that the Maryland side of the river, scarcely half a mile away, was barely visible.

Rayanne stood for a moment in the doorway, feeling the rush of cool air from the building's shadow blowing at the backs of her legs and wondered fleetingly if she should have worn underpants. She saw pay phones off to her left, gratefully on pillars in the shade, their instruments hooded in sterile aluminum, starkly out of place on the 18th century dock, and expensive.

Then there was herself. There was her shift dress. There were her sneakers. That was all she had brought from the studio. No hair barrette, no sunglasses, no purse, no money, no nothing. Nothing, except for the colored post-it with Rayanne's family's phone number. She would have to charge it. This local fifty cent call would end up costing her a dollar at least, maybe more. Shit.

$$* \qquad * \qquad * \qquad *$$

"Hello?" a thin, tired voice answered.

"Is this Elba's mother?"

"Elba ain't here … Can I take a message?" This last had a plaintive, dismissive sound.

"Are you her mother?"

A pause. "Who's calling?"

"This is Rayanne Tellsworth. I'm one of the artists she models … modeled … for."

"I … Harry and me … we don't want to talk to you art people. None of you Art Center people." The phone rattled down onto the receiver and the line went dead.

Shit, Rayanne thought, the police have already been there. I should have known that. Now, she told herself, I'll have to go see them myself.

There was a spot on the edge of the dock where it turned a corner into a landing that was in the shade. She walked wearily over and sat down against a piling, facing the river. She drew up her knees, wrapped her skirt around her, and dropped her head down.

After a few minutes she raised up her head and pressed it back against the soft wood of the piling. She opened her eyes against the bright light and the haze, and realized that someone had come and sat down just a few feet in front of her. It was Jasmine with her feet hanging over the side of the pier, looking around at her.

Jasmine, her eighteen year-old art student refugee from the Corcoran. Jasmine, who pronounced her name Jasmeen and who wanted to be called Jazz. Who almost never spoke to her. Whose work was light fingered and timid, who when urged to paint boldly would make a few wild, incongruous strokes then settle back into her naturally tentative style. Jasmine who should become a maiden aunt and grow old doing pastels on Sunday afternoons.

"Hi, Jazz," Rayanne tried to form a warm smile. It felt awkward on her face. She let it go.

"H'lo," said Jazz. She was looking at Rayanne in a worried way.

Jazz drew up one leg under her and turned more toward Rayanne. "What happened … I never saw anything go down like that before. You know?"

"Yeah," said Rayanne, unenthusiastically. Talking with Jasmine would be an unwelcome strain. She could feel it coming. Plus she would really rather not think about Elba's death right now.

"Me neither," she added softly, hoping Jazz would let it drop.

"Me and her used to do stuff together."

Rayanne looked more closely at Jasmine.

"Really?"

A seagull swooped up from behind the wharf, circled them gaudily then glided lazily off over the water, dropping low over a styrofoam cup then, lifting with a couple of wing beats, turned down river to the south.

Jazz's face was in the afternoon shadow of the building. The two of them were protected now from the sun. Only the heat and the haze remained to remind them of Washington in the summer.

"Yeah, we were in high school together. Robinson, up in Fairfax."

"No kidding?"

"Yeah. We had art class together. Other stuff too."

Rayanne's eyebrows went up.

"Uh-huh. We still hang out together now and then. You know. I mean we used to hang out and all."

"I'm sorry. I didn't know."

"No, I guess not." There was silence for a moment. "No, it's not like we were, like, 'how *are* you,' and 'omigod I'm *so glad* to see you' all the time and stuff like that. It wasn't like that. We just hung out together. You know?"

"Yeah." Rayanne found it easy, this time, to smile. A little smile. It felt warmer.

"She'd wait for me sometimes. After painting classes. I'm slow putting my stuff away."

Rayanne remembered how it did seem to take Jasmine a long time to get her paints and easel put away, and her canvas stowed in the bins. But Rayanne always had the most to do at the end of class so both Elba and Jazz would be gone before she could get away.

Now she framed Jazz in a mental rectangle sitting on the pier, in jeans and a short sleeved shirt, one leg tucked up under her, thick soled, grey streaked sneakers, hair pulled up in a puff held by a wrist-twist. The hands would be the hardest part, she thought. Both hands were in the air. Jazz used her hands when she talked. Little half-jerk, tentative motions, uncoordinated.

"Yeah, I'm slow doin' stuff," Jasmine continued. "She'd, like, wait for me … pretty much every time she was here. 'Nothin' better to do.' That's what she'd say … I'm, like, really going to miss her. You know?"

Rayanne nodded.

Jasmine looked off across the water thoughtfully. Then she turned back to Rayanne. "We even had the same boyfriend, once. I met him first. It was creepy in a way. Davy, you know?"

Rayanne was blank for a moment, then she remembered. Davy was what Jasmine called him. His real name was David-Mark. David-Mark something. But it wasn't his name a person remembered. It was his jewelry. One piece …

"Yeah," Jasmine went on. "He was weird, like."

She brightened enthusiastically. "He had this thing, like? Weird, kind of. You know, like it would … like he couldn't … But Elba's the one talked him into getting it taken off."

She told Rayanne about meeting David-Mark.

It was an open session, meaning no art teacher, just drop-in artists and a model …

CHAPTER 9

▼

DAVID-MARK

"Anybody have a problem with body piercing?" David-Mark asked, hoping it came out not too loud, not too nervous, not too timid.

The man in charge of collecting the money and calling the poses raised his eyebrows. Someone from behind one of the stands called out, "Long as you can hold a pose."

Artists dragged their easels into a close half circle around him, some messing with brushes and ink bottles, some muddling about with pencils, and others fishing their fingers around in blue utility boxes. One young woman, with her hair tied back in a bun and wearing baggy slacks without creases, set out some very deliberate and business-like pastel chalks, arranged in an upright box like soldiers stiffening into full dress for inspection, all lined up by color families.

The head guy said to him quietly, "We always start off with a series of six five-minute poses. Then we go on to one long pose."

The man lifted a beat-up old side chair onto the platform for David-Mark and began smoothing the wrinkles out of a clover green cloth that he had pulled over the chair.

Now was the time to get on with it. David-Mark pulled off his sneakers and socks, standing first on one leg and then the other, and dropped them softly to the floor just behind the platform.

He pulled off his stretched top and turned sideways to the head man's easel, figuring his back muscles would show up nicely in the overhead light. Last he unbuckled his belt and, turning to bend toward them so they would all be looking at his shoulders, pulled off his khaki pants and briefs, knowing that in a second or two they would start looking at his chain.

Released now, after being held against his body heat, the gold chain fell softly and comfortably against his inner thighs. It was a lightweight gold chain with many links and it went right through his scrotum and bumped gently from side to side between his legs as he turned and stepped up onto the boards.

There was a sudden quiet in the room, about the time he felt the feathery links brushing against his skin as the chain uncoiled and as the weight of it caught lightly and pulled at him. Then, like a collective release of breath, there was another sound of easels being moved about, a general shifting of body weights and a loosening and shuffling of drawing tools.

The head guy suggested a standing pose. David-Mark leaned forward, caught the overhead beam with both hands and brought his left heel up in a kind of Achilles-on-the-battlefield pose. It was an easy position to hold. Afterwards came was a fast-paced kaleidoscope of half-sitting, half-reclining poses, then the break before the long pose.

He had brought along an old bathrobe that belonged to someone in his family, he didn't remember whom, because no one in his family had ever worn it that he'd noticed. He covered himself with the bathrobe and cinched it up around his waist.

David-Mark walked around in front of the straggled half circle of easels, some turned left, some turned right, some where people were still working, some abandoned for a cup of coffee in the front room.

A few people said "Hi," some said "Good poses," one said "Good body," and some just nodded and stepped aside so he could look at what they had produced.

They had done an amazing amount of work with the short poses, especially the people working in charcoal. Most had used pencil and barely sketched out his general body shape. One person, a woman, had drawn only his head and shoulders. The mouth was missing but already familiar eyes had begun to look out of the paper at him, and the forehead and hair were definitely his.

He relaxed after the break and was content to let the head guy sort of direct him into a lounging pose, a kind of a Bacchus pose, only not so abandoned, more like a self-conscious artist's pose.

One leg was tucked under. Twenty minutes would probably be pushing it for that leg. It would be dead when he took a break and it would tingle and burn like hell till the circulation came back, but all the rest of him would be OK.

This pose would show his scrotal chain to the easels that stood just to his right of center. He wondered how these artists would handle it.

This time there was noise on a large scale, a shuffling and scraping, as most of the artists changed their positions completely, and dragged easels, stools, papers and drawing tools all about the room till they found their best angles for this pose, the main pose.

At the first break in the long pose, after the head guy and another man helped him mark his position with masking tape, he tried to straighten up, but his dead leg just about gave way underneath him. When he could finally stand on the leg the pain was almost more than he could take. The head guy, who had stood close by to help him up, told him in a low voice next time to flex his leg muscles a little bit now and again. "It'll be all right as long as you pretty much get right back into the same pose."

By this time the break was over. There was a strong coffee smell from the artists who passed close to him going back to their easels. There were charcoal smears on their faces, and pastel marks on their aprons and jeans, and in between their fingers.

During the second break of the long pose, after the artists had logged a total of forty minutes on this position, his legs were functional, thanks to the head guy's advice. He took advantage of his condition to walk around again and see what they had done to him this time.

There were all varieties of media on the easels along the two sides, some ink washes, some chalks, some graphites. Up front in the flatter views all the artists had gone with Pitts, colored pencils on charcoal paper. Some were doing values only—just lights, darks and greys—blocking in the shadows over the angles of his body and between the muscle masses.

One, a young woman wearing a flowered scarf over her head and tied under her chin, must have been a details person. She had gotten his head very accurately, he thought, and then gone straight down the front of him. Now she was roughing in the chair and drape background, making the shadows fall away from the light in a way that looked right to him.

She had been particularly scrupulous, he saw, about the anatomy of his penis and, below in the half shadow, the slight twin bulges of his scrotum. Even this early in her work he could tell that she was going to pick up the specular highlights glinting off his chain.

"I'm Jazz," she said, offering her hand. "What's your name?"

"David-Mark," he said. "With a dash."

"Well, David-Mark-With-a-Dash," she said, "what do you think?"

She had drawn his member sort of chunky and resting partially lifted and outward pointing on the bulge of his scrotal sac, the chain having an almost separate existence in the partial shadow below.

"I thought I sort of hung down straighter."

"You don't," she said, with a flush and a dimple and, turning away, picked up a Pitt.

Later, with easels, oil, chalks, paper and canvases all put away, the artists walked out as a group then broke into couples and trios on the street, headed in different directions. The afternoon sun was hot. Jasmine found herself walking beside David-Mark.

$$* \qquad * \qquad * \qquad *$$

"You know," she said now to Rayanne, as she rose to go, "I remember that I was so distracted, by … you know … the chain. It wasn't till we walked out together that day. Well … he had on a short sleeved shirt … well … he had puncture wounds on his arms."

Rayanne's head jerked up. She stared at Jasmine. "Is he still alive?"

CHAPTER 10

▼

MITCH

Rayanne leaned back against the piling and felt the warm breeze sweeping up from the Potomac brush reassuringly against her cheeks. She raised her arm to squint at her watch without lowering her eyes. Four-thirty. It would not be long till her meeting with Coelho. Why a meeting? What did he want with her?

She had borrowed some money. She'd make another phone call. She slipped off her sneakers and walked barefoot across the dock. Though this time of the day caused the boat dock to be in shadow, the solid, railroad-tie boards were still warm, and she could almost feel the creosote sticking to the soles of her feet. The creosote smell was all about her. There were fewer people now. Probably a lull between the afternoon crowd, with its strollers and young mothers, and the evening crowd with its young adults and dating teens.

"Hello, Mitch? It's Rayanne. Got a minute?" She had a special relationship, she had felt, with Mitchell, the one they all called Mitch now. She had dated him. She could talk to him.

She couldn't remember anymore which of them had asked the other one out. He was close to twice her age, retired government and all that. Not a particularly good painter, or even a zealous one, but he painted with the commitment of a man determined to stay alive and engaged with this world as long as he could drive himself, and she had liked that in him.

On a Friday evening after class, two or three seasons ago, they had found themselves together at The Fish Market, King and Union Streets, directly across from the Art Center and they'd thought it would be fun to order a schooner of whatever was on tap.

It had been fun to discover that they were both sippers, not guzzlers, of beer. Their tall, thin, vase-like glasses had lasted them hours. Their beers had been all warm like the muddy Potomac when you waded among the rushes where the bicycle path to Mount Vernon swung out toward the riverbanks south of Alexandria.

At some point their talk had turned to the differences in their ages, something Rayanne had been thinking about from the very first, early in the evening. Probably Mitch too.

He had been the first to personalize the difference, to put it in terms that were serious but that made both of them laugh. "Don't worry," he had said. "You're safe with me. At my age I have to take Viagra to do anything. That means if I'm going to rape you I have to give you an hour's notice."

It had been so funny the way he had said it. Even now she would still laugh at the recollection. Later, Viagra jokes had gotten old and gone passé in the newspapers. But she had thought his quip was fresh and new, and it had tickled both of them. It had made them both cozy and comfortable in the glow of their friendship.

It had seemed an uncle-niece sort of thing, as if there would never be and never have to be an interlude between the sheets. It had been as if every meal was always dessert, no need for appetizers, no overeating on main courses, no waste of calories or worry about waistlines from meat and potatoes. It was all reward and no work. All anticipation and all fulfillment, with no heavy investment.

The difference in their sexes had been a catalyst for conversation and a basis for their different points of view, rather than a chemical reaction, much less an explosion between them. Getting together seemed like a joy all by itself, but in the end it was sex that kept them together. The beauty of sexuality that figured in drawings and painting, but as the undercoat, the connective structure of a work of art, not the objective of it.

The art that they produced, their drawings and their paintings, they came to realize because they were free to examine this special relationship, were built upon sex but not about sex. It was an important difference that they rejoiced in, that colored and gave life to their hours together. It was no more than natural that at some time, on one particular day, she had happened to ask him if he carried his pill with him or if he left it at home.

What a coincidence, they had both noticed later, that that particular day had been the day he had gone by the pharmacy to have his prescription renewed. It had taken him so long to use up the first 30 tablets that his HMO had finally, grudgingly agreed to pay for the Viagra.

His had been one of the holdouts, one of the last medical insurers to agree to pay for what its hidebound, Bible-thumping management had considered just another type of designer sin tablets. Held out, that is, till even the most reactionary legislators had to admit that the testimony of marriage counselors and the statistics were chorusing the same marriage-saving song.

Yes, what a coincidence. And it had somehow seemed the natural and obvious thing to tease him into taking the pill. "Show me," she had said. Or maybe it had been, "No way, I don't believe this."

In any case he'd popped one in, right then. It had been a normal part of the conversation, just as if she'd said "How are you," and he had answered "Fine, how are you?"

It had been a segue that surprised neither of them then, but now, after all these months, because, to tell the truth about it, people do get used to things, and people do know what to expect of things, and people do recognize the signs of things, she might have felt a life-preserving reflex to stop him.

But then, on that day, it had been natural to watch him take the pill and to laugh conspiratorially, and it had been equally natural to be sympathetic and to say something like "Now you're in for it," or "Now you'll have to do something about that," and to suddenly feel involved and motherly or sisterly or responsible or something. Somehow to feel as if she and he were connected in this act of pill swallowing and that her part would come next, the accommodator, the facilitator, the collaborator, the partner.

They had both been intrigued by the equally fortunate coincidence that her combined studio and apartment was practically next door, which was a good thing, Mitch had said, because the medicine took effect in an hour but no one had ever told him how long before it would wear off. So it had seemed that they had had to hurry and pay, and gather up his artist's folder and her coffee pot which she had been taking home to clean that day and hurry around the corner and halfway down the block to her place.

There may have been some guilt, too. Hell, there was a lot of guilt. A feeling that she had caused it to happen, that he had had to burden himself in this way because somehow she had brought him to the point of doing, or having to do, this. Who knew? Anyway, what was done, she had felt, had been done and the proof was in the way they had hurried along to her place, both out of breath and laughing.

His upper body, with the grey chest hairs, had not been a surprise to her. After all, he had filled in a few times when their model had been late. Not doing the full nudes but posing shirtless for upper body work. He had been the surprised and pleased one. He had been glad to demonstrate.

Though she herself had posed for the class in leotards it had been her policy never to pose unclad for her classes. She maintained an arm's length relationship with her students' work, a connection that seemed to her more professional, one that preserved the respect she wanted to maintain in her classes. And, probably more importantly, she had not wanted to see herself appearing in bad art.

It had all been perfectly natural they both said, for that particular day. Now and again other perfectly natural moments had come and gone. For the most part, though, it had been the uncle-and-niece-with-common-interest-in-art scenario that, for them, had predominated. And it was as niece to uncle she was calling him now.

CHAPTER 11

▼

NOOR

"It was the puncture wounds," Rayanne said with conviction to Verajean. "When we turned Elba over. She had the same puncture wounds on her arms. The same as Carlene's. That's when I knew she had been murdered."

Rayanne and Verajean were sitting at a picnic table outside The Strand, on Union Street. The Strand was Rayanne's favorite takeout eatery in Old Town Alexandria. They made their own bread there and the smell alone was enough to draw you in. It smelled so good at The Strand. The subs they made were gustatory miracles.

A miracle was what she needed right now. Mitch had not been able to help her. She so desperately needed to talk to someone. Especially after Coelho had laughed at her notion about murder.

Well not laughed, exactly. What he really said went something like, "You're not serious, Lady? She jumps up in front of seven people? Seven people all watching her, she jumps out of a window? Come on, now. That's suicide, Lady. Next thing you're gonna be telling me your other nekkid lady … one that hung herself? … in your locked bathroom? … was murdered, too. Get real."

Now she told Verajean, "Coelho didn't believe me. I'm glad you could get out today. I've been feeling like I've got to do something, but I don't know what. I just had to talk to you."

"I've been wanting to talk to you, too, Rayanne. I've got to tell somebody. You won't believe all the red tape I've been through."

Red tape? Rayanne had a little trouble focussing on the idea of red tape. She was still full of the death scene—Elba's wonderful body all flattened and ugly—and the Alexandria police's yellow crime scene tape, not red, strung around the broken glass and everything. Like some surreal three dimensional picture frame experience. Like that artist what's-his-name's plastic wrap draped over the California hills.

"Red tape?" she asked Verajean, not sure how the notion of red tape fitted in.

"Yeah. I've been trying to tell you. I'm changing my name."

She went on, "I spent all day yesterday down in the District. Driver's license. Voter registration. Birth certificate. You even have to go before a judge. A bureaucratic nightmare! Part of Mayor Marion Barry's legacy, I bet you."

"Changing your name? Why?"

"Rayanne, in case you didn't notice, I'm starting a new life. Don't you remember?"

"Well, I remember the part about your new … partner. And about leaving Mikey Joe …"

"Michael," said Verajean.

"Yeah, Michael," said Rayanne, "but why change your name?"

"You'd understand if you were in my place."

Rayanne had no choice but to let that pass. It was like she had never known Verajean. She searched Verajean's face, the dark eyes, the firm, angular jaw. Verajean's hair, newly cut, was short on one side, like a crew, and long on the other side, like a Page Boy. An electric look.

"My new name is Noor."

"Noor?"

"Yeah, it's my hairdresser's name. She's from Afghanistan.

"Noor? Like the Shah of Iran's wife?"

"Yeah. Only it's the King of Jordan's wife. Queen Noor."

"Yes, but he's gone, now."

"No. The Shah is gone, but the King's still there."

"I mean why pick the Shah's wife's name?"

"The queen's."

"O.K. The queen's."

"Well, it's a pretty name. My last name is going to be … is … Abdul."

Rayanne felt herself shrinking into a long silence.

"Verajean …"

"Noor!"

"Verajean … Noor," Rayanne felt the new word. It was heavy on her tongue. "O. K. I can see Noor. But Abdul. That's short for … Abdullah. Isn't it?"

"So?"

"Well, that's the wrong side."

"What do you mean the wrong side?"

Rayanne took a larger bite of her sub than she had intended. All the taste was gone. She chewed hugely and silently for a minute. She wondered if she and Verajean-Noor had been listening to different radio news stations.

"I mean Abdul, Abdullah, is like a Muslim name."

"So?"

"Well, we're against the Muslims."

"Why?"

"Well, because of Nine-Eleven." Rayanne was thinking that they were also watching different TV channels.

"You mean the terrorists?"

"Yes. The guys that flew our planes into the World Trade Center."

"Well," said Verajean-Noor, "what did you expect them to do?"

Rayanne very carefully laid her sub down on her paper plate. She shoved her Pepsi out of the way, set both elbows on the picnic table and looked intently into Verajean-Noor's face. She had never looked so carefully at Verajean before, but she said nothing.

"I get so mad at this administration," said Verajean-Noor. "They are so ignorant when it comes to foreign affairs. Ignorance makes people arrogant. They trample all over other people. I know."

Tears welled up in Verajean's eyes. Rayanne could not help but stare. Verajean's eyes were a deep brown. An intent brown. More like an outer light brown with a darker brown, almost black underneath. In this light, through the brimming tears, there was such an earnest inner sincerity … Rayanne thought of painting … she caught herself. She waited.

"People think," Verajean went on, as if talking to herself, "that the world began on Nine-Eleven. They act like these terrorists came out of nowhere. Like taking down the World Trade Center just suddenly happened. What really happened was that one day everybody suddenly woke up."

Again no response from Rayanne. She hadn't realized Verajean was so political. Maybe it had something to do with this sexual orientation thing she was going through. She wished it would stop. All of it. Both things—this new political thing and the sex thing, too.

"You don't remember the May before Nine Eleven," said Verajean.

Rayanne shook her head in the silence, eyes still on Verajean. One of the tears had worked its way onto Verajean's cheek. Today Verajean's face had an Asiatic look, her cheekbones high and prominent.

"There was an international conference on racism. I think it was in Spain. Anyway, the Arab states wanted to include Zionism in the list of racist movements that was being drawn up. The U. S. and Israel walked out. Rayanne, they just turned their backs on all those people. Turned their backs and walked away. Rayanne, they didn't even have the courtesy to listen. Such arrogance. Such a slap in the face in front of the whole world. Rayanne, people have pride!"

Rayanne could think of nothing to say.

"Mikey Joe told me," said Verajean, ignoring Rayanne's silence, "when we heard it on the news. He said, 'Our country is going to regret this'. And Mikey Joe was right."

Rayanne had no response to the politics part of what Verajean was now saying, but her heart stirred when Verajean said Mikey Joe. Twice she had said Mikey Joe. Not Michael. Maybe she was going to change back again. Could newly hatched lesbians do that? She tried to smile. She did smile. She felt a sudden rush of warmth for poor, lost Verajean.

But Verajean was not ready to stop. "Then our *brave* President, after flying wildly all over the country for eight hours, looking for a place to hide, after the site had been declared safe, went to New York and announced a war to eliminate terrorism!"

Verajean's voice was rising. There was a restless shuffling sound from picnic tables nearby as people began to gather up their brown bags and edge away.

"The wonder is *not* that we suffered a terrorist act," said Verajean. "The wonder is that we've had so few of them. You always have terrorism when one power is incredibly strong and another is incredibly weak. When the strong won't listen to the weak. Ignore their concerns. Look at the Irish. Eight hundred years of terrorist acts under British rule. Look at the slaves in the South. Any protest and they get beat up on. No wonder they killed an occasional slave owner. Who could blame them?"

Rayanne felt small but wished now that she was even smaller. Small enough to be invisible. People around them were leaving. As if suddenly aware, Verajean dropped her voice.

"There is hope. That's why I picked this new name. I was going to change my name anyway. It's part of my new life with Sandy."

Rayanne felt glad that there was new hope. They were alone now on the deck of The Strand. Behind Verajean's head she watched the Potomac gliding silently by and she wished she were on it. Like it had been with her first husband and their tiny sailboat, *Mugsy*. Happy and oblivious in the sun, a light breeze and just the two of them.

Far away from murders, and Coelho, and Verajean-Noor whose friendship she needed so desperately and whom she wanted to get as far away from as possible right now.

"Yes, there is hope," said Verajean, as if she hadn't paused to take a breath or collect her thoughts. "Remember Cyprus? The Greeks and the Turks couldn't get along. They were killing one another right and left, just like the Arabs and the Israelis today. But along came the U. N. and got everybody talking and they worked things out."

Cyprus? Rayanne thought about it. Cyprus? No, she didn't remember, and neither could Verajean-Noor. They probably hadn't even been born then. She twisted her brown bag into a knot, swung her legs around the edge of the bench and stood up to leave. "I'm gonna have to get back to the studio," she said.

"Wait," said Verajean-Noor. "There's one other thing."

Rayanne looked down at Noor. She ached to be somewhere else.

"What was that boy's name again? The chain guy?"

Rayanne told her his name, "David-Mark. What about him?"

"God, Rayanne!" Noor said. "Don't you ever read a newspaper? David-Mark killed himself yesterday!"

CHAPTER 12

▼

PHIL

Next to the cot where Rayanne slept in the one high-ceiling wood floored room that served as office, studio, bedroom and kitchen there was an improbably old two-burner gas stove in equally improbably good shape. It had huge enamel control knobs shaped like salt shakers and its sole function most days was to heat her water for tea. Today she didn't feel like breakfasting at home.

She had awakened with the urge to get outdoors and away from here. It was an unfamiliar feeling. Usually her studio was the place she fled to, not a place to run away from. But today there was something about the closeness of her classroom studio downstairs and the memory of what had happened there that made her want to be out of the building as soon as possible. Getting dressed was the easy part. There was nothing to throw off except the sheet, and only two things to put on.

She picked up yesterday's dress from off the chair and sniffed at the armpits. It would do. She knelt and dragged a wide flat cardboard box from under the bed. She took out a pair of underpants. This was likely to be a difficult day. She did not want to feel unprepared.

Rayanne looked with dismay at her wretched sneakers and decided she'd wait till the last minute, till she was downstairs at the street entrance, to put them on. She would sit on the bowed, sagging steps worn by over a hundred years of feet going up and down. She would slip her sneakers on or, if she couldn't wait long enough to sit, she would simply drop them onto the sidewalk and scuff her feet into them. Hers were small feet and the feeling of a sneaker's tongue doubled back on itself against her bare skin was really not all that uncomfortable.

She thought about that as she splashed water on her face.

She toweled off, then stopped for a second, holding the towel with both hands against her cheeks. Hiding her jaws this way softened the edges of her squarish face and produced the nice elongated oval that she favored in her paintings. Most of her self portraits idealized her jaw.

She thought of herself like her unused paints, as parts of a work in progress, and her face, it seemed, was evolving away from square toward oval. She liked to stay ahead of the change in her paintings.

She looked at her coffee cup sitting by itself on the nightclub table with the long sleeved shift draped over it beside her easel. The cup, originally bone white, had the blackish brown look of a dish that had been too often rinsed without intervening encounters with soap. It was the cup's own fault. There was no running water in the studio, only the sink in the bathroom and no place to set dishes other than the top of the toilet.

Her hair did not need brushing. Her skin was dry by nature. If her hair didn't look tangled, and if there were no drops of paint showing, it was probably okay. She glanced at the line of bottles of ointments, salves and creams leaning precariously across the space between tub and wall. She had cried a lot yesterday but she hadn't sweated much. She would skip the deodorant.

At the end of the hallway outside her studio there was a door leading to the fire escape. It was on the Potomac river side and had the best view. She opened the door into the sunlight of a bright hazy morning. It was not too cool. Her shift dress would be fine. She closed the door and came back inside to check on Señor Cee's catfood and his litterbox.

She walked down the several flights of soft dusty steps to the front door and stopped on the worn stone step where sometimes rain collected. She scuffed her feet into the limp stubborn sneakers. As she had expected both tongues had doubled over on the tops of her feet. No problem. She would run an index finger down around the lace holes when she got to where she was going. Meanwhile she would just have to endure.

A block down to King Street and a left around the corner brought her to the new Chesapeake Bagel Bakery. A fifty cent bagel would fill her up in the mornings, no more calories than it took to paint. She didn't need a lot of calories now that her bicycle had been stolen.

If she told them at the sales counter that she had forgotten her cup they would give her a coffee at the refill price. From the doorway she could see solitary customers scattered about, reading their papers. Good. That meant there would be a free newspaper for her.

She went inside. There was indeed an open newspaper lying on a table near the front window. The paper had an abandoned look about it. There was also a half-empty paper coffee cup. You'd think people would clear away their trash, she said to herself, meaning the cup, not the newspaper. As she headed for the table to claim the paper someone emerged from the men's room, hitching up his pants.

"Mine," he said.

She veered away, toward the counter in the rear of the shop.

"Hey, Rayanne!" the same man stopped. She turned around, surprised, and met a wide grin. A familiar face. Gee, it was early in the morning, was she going to have to start wearing her glasses? Think, brain, think.

"Why hi, Phil!" Thank goodness, she had connected a name with the face. Thank goodness, too, that it was a current student. She hated running into former students—hated running into anyone, really, before coffee.

"Wanna sit down?"

"Yeah, let me get my coffee first."

"Can I get it for you?"

"Sure, why not? Yeah, a cinnamon raisin bagel and a regular coffee, not gourmet. Black."

"Got you. Sit down and read the paper. I'll be right back." Phil was all cheerful.

Too cheerful for this time of the morning, she thought. Boy, she was not yet with it, she also thought.

The front section of the paper had been turned aside. The Metro section lay open in front of her. Damn, it was a picture of Elba, looking like it had been copied from her high school yearbook, and beside it, separated by a column of text, a distant shot of her nude dead body, out of focus enough to pass the more prurient critics.

There were a lot of words in the article. What in heaven's name could they have found to write so much about? The article was continued onto an inside page. She'd have to read it. There was a tiny, single-column copy of one of her students' drawings of Elba, down near the bottom.

She saw her own name, Rayanne Tellsworth, and later on in another paragraph found herself referred to as Tellsworth. Damn, she really, really would have to read this article. She noticed the continuation line, "See Model, page 5." Damn. Dorothy was not going to like this over at the Art Center. She was definitely going to have to read this article.

Phil came back with a tray. He wore a proud, fatherly look. "Cinnamon raisin, right?"

Rayanne nodded.

"Gourmet blend. I got you a medium, okay?"

She made a smile, not brightly. She hated all their gourmet blends. She got up. "I believe I feel like cream after all. Be right back."

He had turned to page five by the time she got back. She had tipped out just enough coffee to spill in four non-dairy creamers, and her drink looked less like coffee now than ecru-colored gravy.

Phil put his finger on another drawing of Elba. "You see this?"

She bent to look, tipping back her cup so it wouldn't spill on the paper, and burned her wrist instead. "Shit."

She wiped her wrist on her hip. Phil looked up, concerned.

"It's O.K.," she said. "Spilt some."

Then "Oh, God," looking at the new picture of Elba, a traditional and particularly uninspiring pose, poorly composed and wretchedly executed. "That's awful. Where do you suppose they got that image?"

"It's one of mine, Rayanne. From your class."

CHAPTER 13

▼

DRAWING

"Oh, God, Phil, I'm sorry. I didn't mean that the way it came out," she lied. She needed to get out of this hole she had dug for herself.

"I mean it's awful they'd put one of our drawings in the paper like that," she tried. "What I really meant was where did it come from? How did they get hold of it?"

"That detective guy. Coelho his name was. He asked all of us, I guess. I had a drawing with me, one I'd done. He said he'd give it back."

I should have known, she thought. She didn't know Phil very well, but she did know that he wasn't the kind of guy to throw anything away. She was vaguely aware that he'd been retired something like five years but he still came to class with pencils and pens in his shirt pocket that had "U. S. Government" imprinted on them. It would have been just like him to carry around drawings he had made years ago. Thank goodness poor Elba was gone and wouldn't have to suffer the embarrassment of seeing this particular image in a newspaper.

For this pose Elba had been lying on her left side, nude, with her head supported slightly on a pillow, her right elbow thrust out to support her body's slight inclination to the right, her left knee raised toward her shoulders and her right leg on top, allowing her feet to fall into what should have been an artful, repetitive sequence.

Phil had apparently located himself below Elba's feet, so that the most prominent parts of her were the soles of her feet and her hips. That in itself had been remarkable. She had known artists who had remarkably strong distastes for painting the soles of feet, and others who objected violently to even showing them, feeling they were somehow offensive.

This must have been one of the classes where she had been explaining perspective drawing. She usually tried to distinguish for her students between perspective from an engineer's point of view and perspective from an artist's point of view.

It was not an easy concept to get across. First she had to explain what perspective was and that usually entailed getting them to make a basic drawing the way they saw a foreshortened figure, and these were usually pretty bad. Next she would have them make several drawings in strict mathematical perspective. These would typically get more and more exaggerated and were usually equally bad, and it was tough enough to get her students that far.

Finally, she would make them try to scale back the perspective effect to something understated till they came up with a pleasing compromise. This was the most delicate and subtle achievement she ever tried to lead her students to master, and they usually stumbled around a lot trying to get there. It had been so easy for Leonardo DaVinci to do, why did it have to be so difficult for her to teach?

Unfortunately for Elba's memory, Phil had apparently never gotten past the engineering perspective phase of the lesson and had clearly gotten stuck in the exaggeration step. Elba's hips and her feet had been big enough, but in Phil's hand the exaggeration of the feet especially was, she admitted to herself, a monstrosity.

To give the man credit he had picked one end of the model's body to work from. If you're going to do perspective on the human anatomy you have to work from a location where you can at least see some foreshortening. The one position that would not have worked would have been directly in front of the model where her prone body had stretched across his field of vision. So he had to be at least somewhat off to one side or the other.

But this perspective! The close-up feet were so large he must have had his easel a scarce half dozen inches from Elba's legs. Nobody would pull an easel up that close. Rayanne always insisted on room to walk between model and students. Boy, this guy had gone compulsive—really anal, in fact.

But even with that pose and that easel position, surely he had done several drawings? Could he have picked this one deliberately? Had he had no others with him? Couldn't he have done something good for her memory? Hadn't he liked Elba?

Rayanne would like to be smiling right about now. Anything to improve the mood of this breakfast a little bit, but her lips and jaws refused to cooperate. She took a bite of cinnamon raisin bagel with a long sip of what had once been really, really hot coffee. The still warm liquid helped.

She peeked over the cup at Phil.

"Bad deal," he said. "Poor kid."

"Yeah."

He tipped his chair back and pivoted so that his legs stuck out into the aisle. He crossed his legs and leaned toward her, his weight on one elbow. "You want to hear something funny?"

She thought for a moment. She did not feel alert just yet. No, a joke would not be welcome. She shook her head.

He went ahead anyway. "This Elba. In a way, you know, she may be better off."

Rayanne's eyes widened. She kept the cup in front of her chin.

"Yeah, probably she's better off. This thing with Mitch was gonna take her nowhere."

Rayanne set down her cup and stared at him.

"Yep, Ol' Mitch, he was laying that Viagra number on her."

CHAPTER 14

▼

CLAN

"Viagra?" It came out weak.

Phil was no longer looking at her. His eyes had moved from her face to follow two people whose early morning shadows in the doorway had momentarily flashed across the periphery of her sight. She turned to look at what he was seeing.

Good God. It was Eileen and Ginger. She really wasn't ready for all these people. Not this early. Not this morning. She hunched her shoulders and pulled her arms in close to her body, wishing now she had worn something more substantial than this flimsy dress. She stared gloomily inside her coffee cup. If she could have crawled into the cup she would have done it.

She swiveled around to follow them as the women passed their table. Eileen and Ginger must have felt Phil's gaze or Rayanne's. They looked over at the two of them seated at the table. "Hey ladies," Phil called up at them.

They came over. Rayanne did not want to be here. She wanted to be away. Somewhere where she could think about Mitch. Mitch and his Viagra with her. Mitch and his Viagra with Elba. What was happening with her life?

And then ... what was going on right now, this minute, in this coffee shop? Today was not a class day. What were all these people doing here? Is this what she had gotten out of bed for? She tried to smile brightly, warmly at Eileen and Ginger. She felt it was not working.

"Hi, Ray. Phil," said Eileen.

"Phil. Ray," Ginger said.

Phil pulled out chairs for them. They didn't sit yet, but Eileen dropped her purse in the chair to Rayanne's left, the one that faced the front window.

"Good to see you guys this morning," Eileen went on.

"Hey, did you get any rest last night? I couldn't sleep at all," Ginger added.

"Why don't we get our coffee so we can talk?" Eileen asked.

Rayanne felt herself nodding and agreeing to something, maybe just to their going away. Something, anything this morning. Why did everyone have to be so hearty, so loud, so energetic this early in the day?

This morning when they should all be some place else, thinking about Elba dying right before their eyes. Why weren't they off doing something? What was all this coming together shit? God, she thought, I couldn't have gotten a bigger crowd if I'd stood out on the sidewalk wearing a sign.

The women came back with breakfast. Eileen's skin had the bright red glow of someone who might have just come back from running. Her hair was wet and on her tray were a paper cup of coffee in a mesh holder and another large paper cup of water with no ice.

Ginger wore a light brown lipstick and her sandy hair was twisted in a pile above her head. Her nails looked freshly done and she had applied the faintest eye shadow with just the right touch of foundation to lighten the dark below her eyes.

Her hair color was a bright red, unlike Rayanne's which tended to a darker, more auburn look. Whereas Rayanne had freckles, Ginger had none, a comparison which Rayanne hated being reminded of.

Ginger's tray held a medium coffee with cream, a banana nut muffin and the peculiar bagel variation known locally as a bagel knot, made from bagel dough, probably cinnamon raisin in her case, without a center hole, covered with icing. Ginger always ate enthusiastically and maintained a good, if solid, body shape. Definitely fuller than Rayanne's, another comparison Rayanne would rather not notice.

The irrepressible Eileen spoke first. "I don't know about you guys, but I couldn't hardly sleep last night." A murmur from the others, Rayanne's more of a grunt, everyone nodding. "Man, I couldn't help but see her lying on the ground like that. Just kept seeing that same thing over and over."

Ginger had been drinking her coffee in big swallows, had taken a large bite of her muffin, and spoke now with her mouth full.

"Uh-huh. You know," she swallowed and cleared her throat with another swallow of coffee, "this is going to sound strange, but it's like a strong feeling you have. An image you get in your mind. You may think this is sick, but," she looked down at her tray, avoiding their eyes, "it makes me feel almost like I ought to paint it some way or another."

None of the other three spoke.

"Is that weird?" She looked at them.

"Yes, it's weird," said Eileen.

"Is that sick," said Ginger, "or what?"

Again a few seconds of silence. Then Phil said, "Naw, not sick. Maybe weird, a little. But," he leaned back in his chair and stretched, grabbing the back of his head with his hands, elbows out, "I can understand where you're coming from. Hey, it was a big deal thing for all of us."

Yeah, especially for Elba, Rayanne thought. Do we have to talk about it?

Again silence.

Eileen spoke, "Phil, could be you got something there. Those were some powerful images. Her staring at us all wide eyed. Her running at that window. Her busting through the window. And, boy, the way she smacked into that sidewalk. I mean it was bad. It was … really bad." Her voice dropped. She raised her cup and sipped meditatively.

"Yeah, bad," said Rayanne, quietly.

A silence, followed. A longer silence, with coffee cups raised and lowered, thoughtful embarrassed chewing.

"Let's paint it," said Phil, at last.

"Paint what?" asked Ginger, through a mouthful of food.

"We paint Elba. We paint her dying, her death. You know. What it means to us."

Everybody thought for awhile. Rayanne's stomach felt very, very wooden. At last Eileen spoke.

"Now *that* is weird. We do models. We don't do feelings, for Christ's sake."

"Right," said Ginger, after taking a swallow. She had started chewing fast. "Representational, that's what we do. Not abstract. From life. Right, Ray?"

"Yeah, from life," said Rayanne, in a small faint voice. Not from death, she told herself. The cold, hard thing in her stomach had started crawling up into her throat. How do you paint an image of death?

Picasso's *Guernica*?

Goya's vision of the Spanish Civil War?

CHAPTER 15

▼

CHILDBIRTH

Over the telephone Verajean-Noor's voice was anxious, petulant. "Rayanne, I can't talk. I've got a shoot."

"Can't it wait a couple of minutes?"

"Not possible. It's my first childbirth. It could be any minute."

"I'll make it quick. Remember those three kids?"

"You're talking about the suicides. We went through that yesterday."

"They were murdered."

"Let it go, Rayanne."

"They all had something in common."

"Yeah, they were artists' models and they needed the money."

"The puncture wounds."

"You said that."

"Yes, but suppose they were all murdered by the same person."

"Some nut going around making puncture wounds on people?"

"Right."

"Rayanne, you're weird."

To herself Rayanne thought, you should know about who's weird. Aloud she said, "They each wanted to be loved."

"Don't we all?"

"I mean they were always so happy to pose, I mean so glad to be with us."

"Rayanne, they were kids without jobs, they needed the money."

"No, really, suppose it was somebody they liked."

"Weird."

"Do you believe that somebody could kill somebody else, without meaning to? Like they loved them and didn't mean to kill them?"

"Can't talk any more."

"Don't you care, Verajean?"

"The name is Noor, and I do care. I'll tell you all about it when I get back."

Rayanne wanted to think about this, but Verajean-Noor was making hauling and stuffing noises in the background. She blurted out, "I read a newspaper today."

"Which one?"

"*The Washington Times.*"

"Wrong paper," said Noor, and hung up.

*   *   *   *

"Look at these games!" said the midwife. "Can you believe it?" Dolores Montoya waved a tiny thin hand at the array on the dinette table. "Monopoly, Scrabble, Parcheesi, and Lord knows what." All in stacks of soft, mealy, swaybacked cardboard boxes.

Delores was a petite woman in a loose print dress than came almost to her ankles. Dainty and graceful, with large sad eyes, she had waist length black hair, and moved her small frame with solemn economy. "When she calls me she says 'I'll have games you guys can play while you wait.' Then she tells me how close her pains are and I'm like 'No way we're gonna be playin' no games, you can forget about that.'"

From the living room couch where she sat alone with all her camera gear, Noor could see three women in the dining room. Besides Dolores the midwife, there were the two childbirth coaches—Maurina Peake and her daughter Mandy Ann. Another woman, Jennifer O'Herlihie, was in the closet-like kitchenette out of sight.

Maurina wore blue jeans with a red plaid shirt. A heavy built, tall woman with short dark brown hair showing grey streaks and a broad, friendly face.

Mandy Ann was even taller, with long reddish hair and strong, well filled limbs. Freckled faced in a granny dress with a long apron at war with her knees, she might as well have worn a sign saying "First Time Birth Assistant."

In the next room Karla Untermeyer lay on her side facing the windows, her backside toward them, a frayed bathrobe vaguely draped over shoulders and hips.

Mostly she was bare and most of her was outside her robe, breasts heavy, legs skinny, stomach stretched tight. Mostly she was too warm. Her feet were on top of the sheets in enormous moosehead house slippers. At this time of year the apartment was heavy with too much heat.

Noor pulled off her vest, leaving just a light weight blouse, which helped cool her upper body, and thought about removing her shoes to help cool her lower body. The other women seemed warm, too.

The midwife opened a window. Welcome cooler air billowed into the living room, a make-do room with a single frayed chair, stuffing showing through, a sofa missing one cushion, and a large-screen television standing like a platoon sergeant at the head of a line of stereo components.

From the bedroom came Karla's suffering voice, a faint whimpering plea for more almond milk. Jennifer O'Herlihie called back to her from the kitchenette behind them, "Jus' a sec."

Jennifer was also pregnant. Also late term. Also breech. And her first baby, too. She was here not just because she was curious. She was here because she was anxious. Anxious and aching. Aching to find out, to see, and to be afraid, if it should come to that.

Jennifer's hair was pure black, and coarse, falling loose to her shoulders. She wore maternity jeans with an elastic pouch in front, and a light blue smock over the top. She sweated in the kitchen steam, and acted like she also wished the apartment was cooler.

Noor thought about photographing Jennifer, too. As long as she was here and had her camera set up.

Against one wall of the living room wall each woman had deposited what she had brought along. As if by prior agreement each had carried in with her a soft, limp bag of essentials. There was the midwife's kit, with thin latex gloves, baby pads and stethoscope. There were the childbirth coaches' pouches, with books and herbal teas and more baby pads.

Then there was Jennifer's duffel, a more random affair. It contained a pillow—in case she had to stay overnight—synthetic against her allergies. Wool socks for if it got really cold, a condition she probably hadn't felt in months. A dress, her only other print maternity dress that fitted, in case there was blood. And a box of soy milk, because Jennifer and the two coaches were vegetarians. Karla, lately introduced to all of them, was a step ahead. She was living the vegan life. No animal nothing, not even butter or milk.

Dolores, the midwife, was comfortable in the outspoken near-militant world of vegetarians. Homebirth advocates tended to be firmly committed to lifestyle.

Their children these days were for the most part home schooled. As for herself, in matters of diet, politics and childrearing, Dolores was, as she said, "… flexible, just plain flexible."

What Karla wanted now was almond milk. You give a homebirth mother what she wants, Dolores had said. Jennifer, the also-pregnant, found the almond milk in Karla's refrigerator. She cleared a space on the kitchen counter by the sink, shoving aside mushroom bits, fragments of asparagus stalks, apple cores, paring knives, saucepans and mugs awash in puddles of cold tea. Between jars of herbs for steeping aromatic teas she set a jogger's water bottle, filled it from the limp plastic-coated carton of almond milk, and screwed on a lid with a plastic straw. Noor captured a few images, using high speed tungsten film with no flash.

"Oh, that tastes so good!" Karla moaned, rolling her eyes, and smiling weakly at Jennifer. She raised herself on one arm to get a better position and sucked noisily at the straw. "I thought my contractions would hurt. I knew they'd hurt. Just never dreamed they would hurt this much." She winced at the memory, then another pain caught her and she moaned for real, flopping the bottle dramatically onto the night stand, and dragging her wrist across the mattress to half lift her weight off the bed.

Mandy Ann, the apprentice coach, had been listening for the contraction. She came barefoot from the dining alcove and climbed up onto the bed behind Karla. "Tell me where," she said.

"Here."

Mandy Ann began to knead Karla's thighs with her fists in the spot where Karla had said.

Noor took a picture of that.

"Hey, Karla, now … think about your baby … I want you to think about how pretty she's going to be … think about what a good mother you're going to be … think about little Monty … think about what a good mother you will be to her … think about all the wonderful things you will do together … Montana is such a beautiful name for a little girl."

Fist downstroke, fist downstroke, with every downstroke something new for Karla to think. Something new to distract her. Think about this, Karla, think about that, they told her. Noor took some more pictures and then reloaded. She carefully stowed the exposed film in her metal box with the air holes in it.

Karla's one extravagance for this baby had been a sonogram. They all knew to expect a girl.

"… you and your darlin' Monty will have such a happy life together … think of how she will look at you … how she will want to be held by you … think of ..." She massaged lightly and slowly, downstroke, downstroke, following the rhythm of Karla's pain.

Mandy called out to the others, "She says she's double peaking."

▼

CHAPTER 16

DOUBLE PEAKING

Double peaking. This sounds promising, Noor told herself, and snapped another frame by way of encouraging Karla.

"Won't be long now," said the midwife. I'll check her when she's resting. Less than an hour, I think. She's doing okay."

"She wants to go to the bathroom." Mandy leaned out of the bedroom.

"Sure. Whatever she feels like. I'll check her when she's back in bed."

A forlorn draped triangle on thin legs with moosehead slippers darkened the hallway. "You guys find everything you need?"

Karla looked so pitiful that Noor could not bring herself to record this particular vision of Karla for posterity. At least not at this moment.

"Don't worry about us. We're fine," said coach Maurina. She waved a mug. "Good tea."

"Thanks," a quick wan pain of a grin, and Karla shuffled into the bathroom. She tossed the bathrobe aside and lowered herself onto the toilet. She tried to drink from the plastic straw. Mandy followed her in and began to rub her neck and shoulders.

"No! Oh, no! Just let me be for a minute."

"Hey, okay. All right. No problem."

The phone rang.

"Can you talk to your mother?" Maurina called from the kitchen.

Noor was beginning to feel lost, like in the middle of a three ring circus with no ringmaster.

"Yeah, tell her to hold on." Karla dragged her mooseheads back into the bedroom, no clothes on, breasts tight and full, hanging heavy on her huge swollen stomach. Mandy followed with the bathrobe, and helped prop her up on pillows. Karla struggled to get comfortable.

Now Noor felt a picture would be appropriate and framed one with as much sympathy as she could muster.

"Yeah, Mama? ... I'm fine ... Not long ... No, not long now. Yeah, he was here ... No, he couldn't stay ... Said he'd call later ... He will, Mama ... Yeah, Mama ... No, I know he will ... Yeah, he will, Mama. He said he would ... He didn't know how much ... I will, Mama. Yeah ... O.K ... You, too ... Bye."

Karla handed the phone to midwife Dolores and flopped back onto the pillows. All four of the other women had followed her into the bedroom. Noor stood back out of everyone's way, in one corner.

"Can you believe that?" asked Karla, "My mother. She's worryin' about child support. She says 'Make him pay that child support, Honey'." This last part she said in a mocking, whining voice, twisting her mouth and rolling her eyes.

Karla rocked her shoulders heavily toward the wall and rolled her hips away from them. "He *said* he's going to pay. What can I do about it now? I'm having a baby for God's sake. My own mother! Lot of help she is."

Noor thought this backside angle of Karla's body looked poetic and took another picture.

"He will love this baby," Karla turned her head to look at them, then dropped her head back theatrically onto the pillows. "He will love my little Monty, our little Monty. I know he will. He will love his little girl." She closed her eyes, thrusting out her jaw against another the pain.

Maurina helped Mandy Ann to massage Karla, sitting on the side of the bed so that her own shadow blocked the light from the window, working on Karla's back. From where she had crawled full length onto the bed Mandy drew up her legs and, in a half reclining position, worked on Karla's thighs. Noor bent down to get a good composition, Karla raised a hand for them to stop, before Noor could get the image right.

"I'm double peaking now," she said. She had closed her eyes in memory of the pain. She was speaking to no one in particular.

Noor made a close-up of Karla's face. She felt good about Karla's eyes.

"Yeah, I know," said the midwife. "If you're ready now, I'll check you." She drew on thin rubber gloves, and inserted the fingers of one hand into the soft dampness between Karla's legs. In her other hand she held a sterile cloth. Karla's knees were up, feet apart. She tipped her head back and grimaced. Great image, Noor thought.

"Good God! What the hell are you doing?"

"Just looking at things. You're dilating just fine. Won't be long now. You can sit in the tub if it will feel better."

"Yeah, anything." She leaned, this time, on Mandy's arm, going into the bathroom. Maurina balanced the faucets to "good-and-hot but not hot-hot," as directed. It was crowded in the small bathroom, the three of them and Karla's big stomach. Noor looked in from outside the door.

Mandy helped Karla into the tub. In less than a minute the next pain came. Mandy laid a towel over the soap tray so Karla could lean against the wall, and gently rubbed Karla's shoulders again, making small circles near her lower neck. In the rising steam Karla's blonde hair curled and pasted itself brown against her bare neck. Noor wiped beads of moisture off her lens.

Another pain. Karla leaned away from Mandy and hunched down till it passed. The phone rang again. Maurina left the others in the bathroom and went to answer it.

Without raising her head, staring down at the water, Karla said "It's him. I know it is."

It was.

"Yeah, tell him to hold on," to Maurina's question from the bedroom. "I'll be there."

Mandy helped dry off her legs and hips, and all that had gotten wet. Karla left her frayed robe in the bedroom. Mandy followed along behind her, dabbing at wet spots she had missed. Noor ratcheted up the shutter speed, opened the lens wider and made an in-motion image, hoping the grain would hold.

"Yeah, I'm glad you called … No, I'm fine … Yeah, Dolores's here … You know, my midwife … That's right, you met her … Yeah, and Maurina and Mandy. No, you know, my childbirth coaches … Yeah, coaches … Yeah, from the Bradley childbirth class. I told you about them … Yeah, that's the ones. And Jennifer O'Herlihie … Yeah, well she's just another client of Dolores's. You know, like me … Well, honey, she's breech, too, and Dolores asked if she could come and see what it was like—no, that's all … And a photographer. A woman." Karla looked up at Noor as if for verification.

Noor nodded, unconsciously.

"No," she went on, "it's not a zoo. I promise you, it's not a zoo. Because they want to help me, that's all. No, I didn't mean it that way … Honey, I love you.

You know I love you … O.K.… Well, I don't know when. Dolores says 'soon' … No, I'm naming her Montana, you know, I told you … You know why … Sure, when you get off … Well, call me … I love you … Yeah, g'bye."

She had squeezed out the last words through clenched teeth. There had been another contraction. After it passed she said, "He forgot. Can you believe that? We met in Montana, and he forgot … I can't believe it. He forgot. What an asshole."

She said it to all of them, standing around the bed, a forlorn look on her face. A little girl forgotten, once again. In the long silence Noor clicked off another one.

Dolores inhaled a quick, loud breath, "I want to listen to the heartbeat."

She pressed the black stethoscope against the lower end of Karla's bulging stomach. "Okay … yeah, okay." It was a cold instrument with the usual ear pieces and a black rod about ten inches long ending in a cup that she pressed against her own forehead while she held the pickup end on Karla's skin. "Okay."

"Now let me check you." She had set aside the stethoscope and was probing with her fingers. "Yeah, she's coming down. I can see an arm. Let me just check. Here."

Another picture. Noor was getting into her groove now. The rhythm of her and her camera, just the two of them, had begun. She was alive now. She and her camera were a team, more than a team. They were one instrument, a single one-eyed image-making instrument.

"Okay. Let me see about the cord. Okay. We're okay here. I'll just move that arm. Just clear that arm."

"Unmph!" said Karla, "Watch it!."

Noor captured that expression. This was photorealism at its best.

"You're doing fine," said Mandy. She was massaging Karla's upper thigh on the side closest to her. "Can I get you something?"

"More almond milk," said Karla. "No, wait. Stay here." She suddenly grabbed at Mandy's sturdy arm. "Oh-h-h. Whoops! … ah-h-h, yeah-h-h-h!." After a long couple of minutes, a weak smile, a very weak smile. "Ooh boy, that was a mean one."

"She's coming now," said Dolores. "I want you to slide down to the edge of the bed. You'll be more comfortable there. Yeah, that's right. Try to brace your feet on the floor if you can. That'll make it easier for the baby to drop."

Karla pulled herself awkwardly with Mandy's help toward the foot of the bed, where Dolores had arranged an old sheet, worn but clean. Another big moment for Noor. She found herself at the end of a roll and quickly loaded more film. Very quickly.

CHAPTER 17

▼

ROUND HEAD

"Maurina?" said Dolores, "How about you getting up here on the bed behind Karla?"

Maurina climbed up onto the bed and crawled around on all fours to position herself behind Karla.

"Yeah, like that," Delores said. "Yeah, legs on either side. That's right. Now slide up close where she can lean back on you. Yeah, Mandy? Yeah, that's right. Put some more pillows behind your mom. That'll give her something to prop up on. It's not long now."

With quick, busy movements she started spreading plastic backed baby changing pads on the floor. Jennifer pulled out some more pads to help.

Another great image.

"Hey, no, Jennifer, I want you to monitor the heart rate."

"Right," Jennifer's voice was tight and faint.

Dolores nodded as Jennifer switched on the fist-sized black box and pressed it against Karla's lower stomach. Jennifer read the LED numbers out loud.

"Yeah, that's good," Delores said.

Then, peering in where her fingers were holding Karla open. "Hey, good. I can see her. Mandy get me that mirror. Yeah, in my bag." Without looking up.

Noor got a picture from the side.

Mandy came back with the mirror, a wooden framed mirror about six inches square with thick rounded edges. Karla reached desperately for the mirror, hand flailing, scattering crystalline rocks off the side table. Mandy caught her hand and closed the fingers around the mirror. Karla pushed it down between her knees. Her movements were jerky now and anxious. "Yeah, I see. I guess." Noor got the picture.

"Here, take it back," said Karla. Mandy grabbed for the mirror as Karla let it go.

"Okay. Now, when I tell you to push, I want you to push," said Dolores. "Really push."

Karla nodded grimly. Mandy had wet a towel and touched Karla's forehead.

Karla leaned into the damp, hot towel as if for comfort. She tensed, her lips wide with pain. Maurina was still behind her, supporting her weight. She clenched at Maurina's knees on either side of her hips. She had kicked off her house shoes and was naked on the edge of the bed leaning against Maurina, hot and sweating.

Noor got another one, this time from a distance, taking in the whole bed and everyone on it.

"This next one's it," said Dolores. "When it comes you got to push. You got to push hard."

Karla braced. On command she pushed. She tried to look down at her crotch but her head had to stretch back, had to. Her head rammed up and back onto Maurina's ample breast. Karla was hurting. Too much pain to look and push at the same time. After the contraction she looked. She burned. It was a fire between her legs, she moaned, like a bright razor stinging cut and a bonfire all at the same time.

Karla snatched at Mandy's mirror.

Noor got behind Karla so she could see into the mirror too, her camera's viewfinder to her eye. What she saw was large and grey and wet with matted black flecks. She also saw Dolores's fingers underneath. The fingers were inside of Karla, too, supporting the lump of the baby, guiding it. Noor took another picture. The whole damn world was crammed into Karla's crotch.

"O.K. The next one's the big one. Get ready." Dolores braced her body, hands tight. Noor scrambled around so she could focus on the action area from in front.

The next contraction came. The burning was volcanic. Karla twisted her head to the side in agony. She opened her eyes and looked down. About eight or ten inches of new baby was squeezing out butt first, between her legs, its weight supported in Dolores's hands. Noor got the image.

Another contraction. Karla pushed again. More burning, it seemed. Maybe not so hot as before. How could she tell, Noor asked herself. She must be on the same wavelength with Karla, maybe they all were.

She snapped another one. Montana was out.

"See? Perfect little round head!" said Dolores. All triumphant she handed Montana up to Karla. "Perfect little round head. I told you. That's what you get with breech babies. A perfect little round head!"

Karla sucked in a quick hard breath. Her eyes wildly, hungrily swung to her baby, fastened on this baby that had come butt, feet and hands first into the world. The body had come out still as death. Noor felt deep, cold fear. Dead?

The baby jerked. She started to squirm and twist and make little snuffling noises. Noor recovered enough to squeeze off another one.

Karla caught at her own breath, spastic, like it would never come back. Quick gasps, rounded sucking lips. Still breathing jerkily she took the baby between her breasts, and held her infant skin to skin. "She's beautiful!"

Noor memorialized the moment.

Mother and daughter were still connected. The long, kinked grey-purple cord dangled from Monty's tummy to Karla's vagina, where her legs hung open, feet on the floor, her back resting against Maurina's chest. Noor clicked off another image and it burned into her brain.

Then, with one hand propping little Monty secure between her breasts, resting atop her stomach big with the placenta still inside, Karla grabbed at Dolores's arm with the other hand and grinned a sweaty grin up at all of them. She nodded down at Monty. "You were right," she said to all of them as she looked at the child on her stomach, "a perfect little round head."

Noor took one more picture. It was time to get out of there. Too many women, too much women's stuff. She began gathering her gear into the living room.

"Noor. Noor!" It was Karla in a whiney voice. "Come to Monty's christening, will you? I want you to do the pictures."

"O.K." Noor was reluctant. She was sick and tired of all these women and all the sweat and the pain. She really didn't want to have to deal with them again.

But, she would get even with them. She would take Rayanne with her.

CHAPTER 18

▼

ON POSE

"Rayanne," asked Noor, "how long have we known each other?" It was the day after Noor's breech birth shoot.

"I don't know," said Rayanne thoughtfully, as she slowly laid her shift dress over the back of a chair. She kicked off her sandals. Her toenails were painted alternate pinks and purples. "Must be five years. Maybe six. Why?"

"How come I'm always posing for you?"

"Why not?"

"Well, this is the first time you've ever posed for me."

"Beats me," said Rayanne. She tugged at the waistband of her panties and see-sawed her hips and her knees so that they dropped down around her ankles, then lifted them off with the toes of her foot and tossed them to the side. She wondered, are my hips still growing?

Aloud she said, "Posing for a painter is easy. All you have to do is show up." She giggled, "That's why I picked you for my model every time I couldn't get anyone else. You had the right talent for the job!"

Rayanne had thought they were good enough friends for her to tease Noor. In the silence that followed she almost panicked.

Then Noor laughed. It was a good, hearty, belting laugh.

Rayanne had always liked Noor's laugh. She liked a lot of things about Noor, and about being with Noor. Noor had a good body that she kept hard with daily workouts down at Gold's gym. Her hips were slim for her size and her breasts were high and taut, like a female bodybuilder's before implants. Really there were no spare ounces of fat anywhere on her.

She knew that Noor's body looked sleek when at rest, sleek and feminine, in a brusque sort of way, but when she pumped up she could produce rips and splits. It was a miracle to watch. Sadly, the nature of working with the painting medium meant Rayanne had never been able to capture that magnificent muscle definition on canvas but what they had done together with Noor's brooding, troubled feminine intensity had been good enough, and Rayanne had been more than satisfied.

Now, for the first time, it was Rayanne's turn to be the model.

Rayanne had been amused, when they started, at how much preparation time went into setting and resetting, checking and rechecking the props, the shadows and the lights.

For Rayanne's own work behind the easel, two lights pointed in the model's general direction was good enough. Now, on the other side of the reflectors, she listened with amusement to Nora's mutterings about broad light, key light, highlights, back light and reflections. What a to-do about reflections—baffles, scrims, flags. It went on and on. Too many details to think about. Besides, Rayanne had other things on her mind.

"Noor," she asked, "do the murders bother you?"

"Not any more."

"What do you mean, not any more?"

"Because they're not murders. They're suicides. The Alexandria Police said so."

"They're saying so doesn't make it so."

"So you're going all philosophical on me?"

"No, I'm just telling you what it looks like to me."

"Are you better than the Alexandria Police?"

"You mean you're siding with them?"

"It's not a matter of siding with anybody. It's plain as plain can be. You saw Elba kill herself. How much plainer do you need?"

"Noor, you know Elba wouldn't do anything like that!"

"Doesn't matter what *I know*. What matters is what *you saw*. What did you see?"

Rayanne stared at her friend and began once again to feel lonely, very, very lonely. If this had been her studio she could have heard a clock ticking, but this was Noor's studio and Noor didn't "do" clocks.

Rayanne realized that she had been staring without seeing when she suddenly noticed that Noor was looking hard at her, a small frown wrinkling the side of her forehead that had the crew cut.

"How do I look?" Rayanne felt she had to ask in the silence.

"Too neat," said Noor. "Mess up your hair a little."

Rayanne obligingly threw herself forward, the way she would have done in the days when she had worn long hair, so that it would fling itself over her face and hang down in front. She wagged her head from side to side, then straightened up.

"Not enough," said Noor. "Mind?"

She stepped close to Rayanne. They were both barefoot, which was the way Noor worked in her studio, so that she wouldn't tear the backdrops when she stepped on them.

There was no comparison between their heights, Noor was way taller. She pushed her fingers into Rayanne's hair and rustled them around, like a kid playing in a sandpile. The result, Rayanne could see in the mirror behind Noor, was a mess.

"Don't worry," said Noor. "We're doing mostly body parts, today. It'll be fine."

Rayanne stood, suddenly feeling naked. And small and still.

"Let's spin around and stop. Facing me."

Rayanne did it a couple of times for practice, Noor's camera following her. Then Noor said, "O.K. After you see the flash, do it again. Faster, if you can."

"Yeah ... that's it ... right ... bingo!"

Again and again, till Rayanne was dizzy. Noor was up, shooting down. She was down, shooting up. She was on the left. She was on the right. She was anticipating. She was lagging. Rayanne was getting sick.

Noor ran out of film. Rayanne collapsed on the floor, lotus position, her skin too flushed to be cold.

"Told you it was hot work," said Noor, "but no, you were afraid you'd get cold."

"Well, it's not like posing for the canvas." She watched Noor re-loading and it seemed her friend was irritated. "And it's not like regular posing for a camera, either."

Those must have been the right words to say. Noor brightened. "If you want pictures that look like just anybody's then go to just anybody," Noor said, and seemed pleased with herself.

This has got to be the right time, thought Rayanne. Aloud she asked, "You know what I'm wondering?"

"Uhn uh."

"Remember those puncture wounds?"

"Let it go, Rayanne."

"Yeah, but they all had 'em."

"So?"

"So, what if they killed themselves *because* they had puncture wounds?"

"Why would they do that?"

"I don't know, but what if they did?"

Noor fitted a new lens, and stood up, looking business-like in her creased blue jeans and white T-shirt with the peace sign on the back and the American flag on the front.

"Rayanne, there's no telling what somebody will do if they want to kill themself bad enough."

This was not going in the right direction. Rayanne tried anxiously to find another way to say what she meant. She felt skinny sitting on the floor. The bare boards were hard against her bones, as if she had no flesh to pad her. Noor interrupted her thoughts.

"What did Coelho say about the holes in their arms?"

"He said," she twisted her lips and made a nasal sound, "'That's a nice try, little lady.' I hate it when somebody calls me little lady. He said 'It's probably a cult thing. It don't change anything. A suicide is a suicide is a suicide.' I guess he thought he sounded literary. He's a horse's ass."

"He's right, though. A suicide *is* a suicide."

"I don't care. I'm going to see for myself."

"See what?"

"I'm going to see if there's a cult."

"You mean a bunch of people with holes in their arms?"

"Yeah."

"Good luck. You're just one person. A detective with a conté crayon. What can you do that the whole Alexandria police force couldn't do?"

"I don't think anybody but Coelho ever looked into it."

"I doubt that."

"Noor, are you my friend or not"

"What's that got to do with it?"

"I may need you."

"Right," said Noor. "Meanwhile, let's get back to work."

Noor pinched her chin between thumb and forefinger, then added, "... let's do feet. I love feet."

A pause.
"Up on your toes, little lady."

CHAPTER 19

▼

YELLOW TAPE

"Let it go," was the same thing Detective Coelho said. "Let it go. We did an autopsy, just like you wanted. A little of this, and a little of that. Yeah, she was trying stuff. But not stuff makes you jump out a window. My advice? Just let it go."

It was late evening with long yellow rays glinting on rising, dancing dust motes through Elba's window. It would always be Elba's window now. Coelho sat facing Rayanne in a corner of the studio where unused stools and easels were stacked. He had insisted that the stools at the easels be left untouched. "People don't do that kind a' shit, that kind a' stuff, to theirself," Detective Lieutenant Coelho was looking at her, but Rayanne's eyes kept dropping away in her misery.

Looking at the floor would not make the image of his face go away, however. In her mind's eye she could still see his dark skin, small head with high cheekbones, hollow cheeks, prominent nose hairs, pencil thin moustache, shiny black hair, collar open at the throat, no tie. He had dropped his dark grey suitjacket over a stool to his right. It did not match his pants, which were brown.

"How 'bout clowning around, you know, goofing off? Like acting silly? Kind a'-, you know, to make other guys laugh at her. She do stuff like that?"

Rayanne gave a quick little shake of her head, wretchedly hunching her shoulders, looking at the floor.

"Naw," he shook his own head. "Same thing the others said. Funny."

Then, "You know how artsy people carry on, doing weird stuff."

Rayanne lifted wet swollen eyes to him, puzzled.

"You know. Different. Not like normal people."

Her eyes widened. "What?"

"You know. Like strippin' in front of people. Like she was. You know. Nek-kid."

The door was closed. Locked. The yellow tape remained, the letters "ALEX PPD" chasing each other along the ribbon as if caught in a strobe light. Visually quite remarkable in the narrow hallway. Rayanne put it in the back of her mind with other conceptual cues and visual fragments. Maybe the beginnings someday of a powerful abstract, or a canvas with a hard emotional theme.

"The way it acted on her, the amount she had in her system, had to a' been in her water bottle. She had to a' drunk it a little while before she took the dive," he said, and paused, "Ma'am."

Then, "Okay if I call you Ray-Annie?" He stretched it out.

Ray shook her head.

He must have thought she meant no problem. "O.K. then, Ray-Annie. This Melba …"

"Elba," Rayanne's throat wanted to swell. She needed to unblock her throat so the tears could flow, but she forced the words out so the tears wouldn't come. "She didn't do drugs."

If she could help it she wouldn't invade Elba's privacy or let this man either, this little man, barely taller than her, with small dark eyes and hollow cheeks. Elba had lived in a house with other young singles more or less all of whom had modeled for Rayanne and for the Art School at one time or another, supporting themselves otherwise mostly by waiting tables, none of whom knew more than a couple of days ahead whether they'd be available. He'd have to find out that part from somebody else. Her throat tightened again, the fire flared her cheeks. Hot tears began to run.

"Somebody done her then," he went on. "Figures. If she'd been clowning around she might have fallen out backwards, but she wouldn't a jumped out. On the other hand, she'd a' been a goddamned exhibitionist, she'd a gone out buck nekkid, like she wouldn't a' wrapped a bath robe around her."

"Plus," he was thinking out loud, "if she'd tripped or something looks like she'd a tried to save herself. Grab at the window, get her arms under her, protect her face. Something."

Rayanne hunched her shoulders and bobbed her head up and down, staring into the darkness of her circling arms.

"Could a' been you," said Coelho. "But I can't think why. Or one of your students. Nope, can't say why. Really dumb thing to do. Shitty, too."

He told her he'd checked how many years she had used Elba. He knew she'd told the class the previous week that Elba would be their model, so all who were there that day had a week to figure out how to "do" her.

He was not ruling out the two men. Both had left early but not so early they couldn't have doctored Elba's water, but more people around would have meant "... more likely somebody'd a' noticed. Turns out all of them knew this Elba gal before."

Yes, Rayanne had had all of them at one time or another in an earlier class and she always used Elba at least once a semester. But why was he telling her this? Elba was a good person, with a wonderful body type. Would he care? This killing part she didn't need to hear. She wiped tears with the palms of her hands, fingers up, like licking after ice cream.

"Could be either of them guys, foolin' around a little on the side." He was looking earnestly at her. She barely saw the detective through the filmy dampness. She gave up wiping, and sat hunched in her misery.

"Still," he went on, "could 'a been one a' them women. That youngest. Maybe a boyfriend mixed up between 'em?"

She shook her head, meaning she didn't know.

"Prob'ly not. I agree with you there. No competition."

God, how she bristled at that. Men could be so narrow minded.

"Oldest woman, the other hand. Can't figure her. Woman her age, come here to class all these years. Would a' thought she'd a learnt to paint by now."

Rayanne's hands were wet. Her eyes burned. She'd like to hit this man. Right in the face. Hard. And make him go away.

"Said she'd painted that gal off and on. Four, maybe five years. Who'd a' thought it? Must have a thing for fat gals."

Rayanne cupped one hand across her mouth and brushed at the salt in her eyes with the other. Tried to look at him. God! Ignorant bastard!

"Can't figure those other two gals neither. Come to find out they knew her from work."

What work? Maddie and Eileen were housewives. Come on! Was he going to go on forever with this stuff?

He didn't. He simply stood up, let his eyes roam around the room as if he were looking to buy the place, shrugged his shoulders and walked away quietly.

Rayanne, with her head bowed, peeked over the top of her handkerchief. She could see nothing higher than his feet as he walked out the door. Below his dress trousers, she realized, he was wearing runner's sneakers.

CHAPTER 20

▼

ALONE

With Coelho gone and no one looking she pulled up her loose bodice, wiped her eyes and looked around at what he'd left her. The studio, except for his stool and hers, was arranged pretty much as it had been when Elba went out the window. The door was closed, with tag ends of yellow tape showing in the cracks where he'd pulled it shut.

You can help me, he had said, you can make my life easier. You can make this easy for all you people, too. Whatever that meant.

What did he think she knew? Or guessed? What could she possibly know that he didn't already know? She pulled her feet out of the hopeless sneakers and up onto the stool. She gathered the loose ends of her shift around her ankles, dropped her chin onto her knees and balanced there on the small disc of the seat, pulling the thunderous cyclone of her wretchedness inside her.

She was alone in the studio, yellow tape running around the room like a gym decorated for a dance. It was time now to cry. She could feel the tears coming up again. Up from the swelling deep in her throat. She was sorry for Elba. So young. So sweet. She was sorry for Carlene, gone so long ago it seemed now. Sorry for David-Mark, too. She was sorry for herself. She was too young, also, and too lost in a strange world of hateful frightening things that happened to people.

Did someone really cause Elba's death? Did someone murder her? She thought about the "perp," as Coelho had called him … or her. Were there really such people who could deliberately try to cause somebody else to die? She felt all browns and blues inside. She felt all diagonal strokes, all anger and unhappiness, a palette knife making sharp quick jerky lines.

Then, this guy, Coelho. Why had he brought her here to talk without the others around? What did he want with her? What did he think she could do for him? Why not just go away and do his own investigating? Couldn't he just look at his mug shots … or whatever else it was that they did in police stations?

Rayanne fervently wished Coelho would leave her alone. She wished he would go away forever and take this whole horrid thing away with him. She turned to look at the broken window, some pieces still in the frame, other pieces on the floor. There might still be cleaning up outside to do also, she thought.

She wished Coelho would erase her whole memory of this so she could go back to Elba alive and posing again. She looked up at her easel, where she'd been working along with the students and she knew that every time she looked at this work that she had started she would always be reminded of what had happened here. She was glad it was Elba's figure and not Elba's face that was emerging on her canvas, but most of all she wished it were someone else's body today. Maybe she'd tear up this picture and throw it away. Or burn it. She'd never burned a work before. She would burn this one. Yes, she would definitely burn it. Maybe.

It would be easier for herself, Rayanne thought, if she could just die. Just lie down right here on the floor and die. She raked the sole of her foot along the floor, watching the sweat of her skin pick up the powder of dust and leave a light, shining smear behind.

Maybe she'd paint. She might feel better if she painted. Maybe she would start to work colors into this drawing of Elba she had started. Maybe she'd go upstairs and pick up where she had left off with her self portrait in blue. She wanted to do something. But she'd have to get up from here if she was going to do anything.

She shifted her weight and drew the side of her other foot along the floor, in a different place where the dust had not yet been disturbed. She wanted to do something. She wanted to do … nothing. Nothing. Nothing at all.

And she would like to paint herself doing nothing at all.

CHAPTER 21

▼

SATURDAY

"I can't believe this," said Rayanne, grumpily. "It is eight-thirty in the goddamn morning and we are way the hell out in the middle of nowhere."

Rayanne did not do mornings well. It was two weeks after Noor had photographed Karla's breech birth delivery and Noor was driving her to the baby's christening. It was to be held on a horse farm in the Virginia hunt country, somewhere near Middleburg.

On a Saturday morning the traffic on Route 50 west was light, which was a good thing, because Noor was a terrible driver. Her way of passing another vehicle consisted of speeding up till she was almost on the other car's bumper then suddenly swerving into the left lane with the accelerator to the floor, flying past her adversary, twisting the wheel to the right to put them just ahead of the startled driver's front bumper and hitting her brakes. A half-dozen of these experiences and Rayanne was ready to unlock the passenger side door and hit the eject button.

Route 50 was a broad, boulevard-like thoroughfare in the city, but out here in the Northern Virginia countryside Route 50 was only sometimes a four lane road. Other times it was two lanes, running through small woods, and over and around undulating green hills that were also small. The ever present haze pressed in on them, obscuring their view of the distant Shenandoah mountains and imparting a wet surreal glow to the houses and barns they passed.

Rayanne was not a painter of landscapes but she almost could not resist the tug of the weathered reds and rusts of the barns, the grays and browns of the stone fences, the five hundred shades of green in the fields and woods, and the reflections of reeds in the ponds. One pond actually held a swan that lifted its wings and arced them at her as they passed. Half a mile later she realized she was still holding her breath.

Except for these visual flights of fancy her grumpiness had not improved much when they finally turned off of Route 50. Noor slammed the car over to the side, wheels off the pavement, and jammed on the brakes. Rayanne held her tongue while Noor consulted her notes, then started up again.

"I hope they have coffee at this place," Rayanne was still grumpy but Noor was tense, in that pre-hysterical way she always got before a shoot, and Rayanne knew that she herself was going to have to be the one to ease off before they detonated, right there in the car.

"They'll have coffee," said Noor. "They may be Vegans but they're still normal people."

Vegans? Normal? That's an oxymoron, thought Rayanne. Aloud she said, "I don't see any horses."

Noor gave an exaggerated snort that would have embarrassed a horse, but that was her version of a quick laugh, and pointed off past Rayanne's side of the car. Beside them ran a stone fence with a one-slat wooden rail on top. The field on the other side was immense and, sure enough, on the far distant edge, against the trees, were horses, maybe three or four.

"Why so few horses in such a big pasture?"

"Rayanne, why are you so obtuse? This is Virginia hunt country, not the god damned O. K. Corral out west, for God's sake."

The implication was clear. That was all the explanation Rayanne was going to get and she'd have to figure it out for herself. Rayanne decided to live with the mystery. She let it go. She slid her bare feet off the car seat, back into her sandals, and crossed her arms.

After another few minutes of silence, Noor slowed to check the name on a mailbox on the passenger side then pulled into a driveway on the left. The surface of the drive might have been lightly paved or oil-covered at one time but now it consisted mostly of blackish lumps of broken gravel.

The driveway straggled past a collection of small buildings, some of which may have been garages or storage sheds, none of which looked like horse barns, and one of which had a sign over the door bearing the words "Print Shop." Rayanne wanted to ask about this place but neither of them was in a charitable mood this morning and she really didn't want to lay any heavier intellectual demands on her friend than necessary till they had both had some caffeine.

At the end of the driveway, on a rise that overlooked a surprisingly long drop to a distant valley, stood what appeared to be the main house. It looked less like a Virginia estate home than an A-frame summer house with a deck. They parked near the steps. There were no other cars around.

Noor knocked on the door of what appeared to be a combination kitchen and great room. There was way too much glass on this side of the house to suit Rayanne. No one answered the knock though some movement was visible through the window to their right. Noor pushed the door open.

"Verajean!" said Rayanne. Noor looked back over her shoulder. "I mean Noor."

Noor led her on into a living area decorated with crystal rocks and twigs twisted into circles and crosses. Three boys, somewhere around early adolescence, were playing a board game on the crocheted rug that took up half the floor space. There was a TV making noise in one corner. None of the boys looked at them.

"We're here for the christening," offered Rayanne. One of the boys glanced up at her. He seemed unimpressed.

"Where is everybody?" asked Noor in a louder voice. This made the other two boys look up.

"Nobody here yet," one of them said.

We're not nobody, Rayanne told herself.

"You got any coffee?" Noor was a no-nonsense kind of person.

"Yep," said one of the boys and they all turned back to their game.

Rayanne and Noor followed their noses over to the kitchen which consisted mostly of a counter and stools standing barricade-like between the cooking area and the living area. They searched. There were clean cups in the dishwasher.

The coffee was indeed hot and they found milk in the refrigerator. There was no sugar to be seen and even Noor was reluctant to go through the cabinets without permission, so they took their coffee out onto the deck and sat on the steps.

Gradually Rayanne felt herself coming to terms with the less disagreeable parts of the morning. Noor looked at her watch and groaned.

CHAPTER 22

▼

CHRISTENING

"Nine o'clock, they told me," she said. "Now look. It's almost ten."

Rayanne did as she was told and looked at Noor's watch. It was indeed almost ten o'clock. She felt sorry for both of them and for a perfectly good Saturday morning gone to waste.

She lifted her head at the sound of motors and rustle of gravel. Two cars were rounding the print shop and heading up the driveway. They were old models and dusty, but they pulled slowly and grandly, cavalcade style, into spaces among the trees close to where Noor had parked.

There was a big to-do in the vicinity of the left rear door of the lead automobile where the mother of the new baby made a dramatic struggle of climbing out and giving directions about the gathering up of all her baby gear. Rayanne was told this would be Karla, the mother of the about-to-be-christened baby girl, Montana.

Watching all the uproar and already beginning to smell the new baby smells, Rayanne began once again to wish that she were somewhere else and she suspected Noor felt the same way. The only difference was that Rayanne had been wishing it all morning, whereas Noor had been buoyed by the anticipation of a shoot. About now, however, the reality of these people and the banality of this event would be dawning on Noor.

Well, Noor had it coming, Rayanne thought. I could still be in bed.

As women continued to swarm out of the two cars Noor muttered something in a confidential voice about the midwife, the Bradley coach and the birth assistants she recognized.

Rayanne gradually became aware that there was a second eddy of attention swirling around an older-looking woman with a surprisingly erect posture, who emerged from the second car, wearing a celebrity's serene smile.

All the people seemed to be in everyday clothes. They looked as if they had interrupted their Saturday routine just long enough to dash out into the country for a few minutes. Rayanne regretted that she had gotten up fifteen minutes early to root around for an unworn dress that she wouldn't have to iron and for her nicest nearly new sandals. She regretted removing her pink and purple toenail polish. She looked down at her clean feet and bright red sandals and thought … shit.

From the A-frame behind them came the sound of the kitchen door opening and five or six more females, including two little girls, swarmed out and over the newcomers.

Rayanne immediately lost track of what Noor had said about who might have been who. She was already plotting how she would revenge herself upon Noor when the door opened again and a man walked out onto the porch wearing the same sickening look of serenity the old celebrity had shown when she got out of the car. At least "serenity" was the best one-word name she could give to the woman's tentative smile, tinged with a smug disinterestedness. Not exactly a Mona Lisa look, for sure, but something not far from it. She'd think about how to paint that look later.

Rayanne heard the new mother introducing her baby to the man who had just come outside and to the woman who must have been his wife. It seemed as if the baby's mother had been friends of this couple in a previous life, maybe the "Print Shop" sign had something to do with it.

The elderly woman was introduced as Elizabeth, who would be performing the christening ceremony.

No one had noticed Noor and Rayanne. All the commotion had swirled around and past them as if they were no more than chair rails on the deck. Rayanne decided that this man and his wife must be the hosts. She went up and introduced Noor and herself as the photographer and her friend. A quick smile and an "I thought so" from the woman was all she got in return, then the whole crowd focused once again on the mother and baby. The little girls were particularly entranced.

"Very nice farm you have here," said Rayanne, with all the graciousness she could muster. Not only did she not do mornings, she realized, she did not do Saturdays either, or graciousness.

"It's not ours," said the woman, turning away. Then in a louder voice she said so all could hear, "I've got stuff coming out of the oven. Let's all go inside."

I can't believe this, Rayanne thought to herself, now we're going to eat. When in hell are we going to get to the christening? She looked accusingly at Noor. Noor shrugged and they followed everyone inside.

At their hostess's insistence the boys reluctantly placed the pieces of their game on the coffee table, all in a heap, and everyone sort of straggled around the kitchen counter putting samples of this and that into paper plates, helped themselves to coffee in a motley of ceramic cups or, in the case of the kids, orange juice in glasses, and found places to sit, some indoors, some outdoors.

Noor was one of five people wedged into the couch. Rayanne dropped cross-legged onto the floor beside her and smoothed her long skirt down over her knees. Wedging the soles of her sandals underneath her hips forced her ankle bones painfully against the bare floor and she wished she had plopped onto the crocheted rug instead.

The little girls as well as the boys were asked by one or another adult from time to time to bring this or take that and the children all moved, not briskly but obligingly, to do as requested. Everyone's too agreeable here, thought Rayanne. She was beginning to think they were all on medication.

There was talk mostly about the new baby, who was being passed around to everyone except the old woman, children included. Finally, after what seemed forever, the woman who had spoken first to Rayanne said, "If everybody's had enough to eat why don't we have the christening now?"

Surprisingly all five kids starting making enthusiastic noises and the adults got up from their various cushions and arm rests around the room and started stacking dishes and tossing paper plates into a trash basket that had been revealed under the sink, with a dramatic gesture, by one of boys.

At last, thought Rayanne. She was glad to see that Noor also was a little more animated as she picked up her camera bag and followed the others out the door.

"I thought the apple orchard would work," said the hostess.

"That will be nice," said the old woman, Elizabeth, putting on her congenial smile, and congenially was the way everyone followed her uphill to gather beneath the oldest looking apple tree. There they arranged themselves in the sunlight spotting through the branches.

Being an apple tree it had straggly branches offering very little shade, but Noor seemed pleased with the mottled lights and darks it made on everyone's faces and quietly squeezed off a few frames.

Raised Catholic, Rayanne expected religious rites with lots of trappings but she looked about in vain for vestments and candles. On the other hand she had attended many a Protestant ceremony, too, so she was in a position to settle for just a Bible. But there was no Bible in evidence.

"You can hold the baby," the old woman, Elizabeth, said to Karla. "If you get tired, maybe someone else will help you."

It was not a suggestion but an order, an order that all of them felt, even Rayanne.

"The baby's name?"

CHAPTER 23

▼

NAME

"Montana," said Karla, holding the baby up a little so that everyone could see.

The old woman continued to look at Karla, not speaking.

"Montana Louise," said Karla.

This seemed to satisfy the woman. She reached into the pockets of her dress, a dress that hung in long folds to her ankles, and pulled out a twig. "From *my* apple orchard," she said, "just like this one."

She touched the baby's hand lightly with the twig and smiled as the child's fingers curled around it. After a while the baby released the twig and she held it up for all to see.

"This is a sign of life," she said. "Life is all around us. Life is part of us. We are part of life. Life is one."

What's going on, Rayanne wondered. Are we all going to be goddamned Druids here?

The old woman handed the twig to one of the boys and said, "Pass this limb among you. Let everyone touch life. Let life touch everyone."

When the twig came to Noor she took it in two fingers as if holding a soiled diaper and passed it quickly to the person next to her. Others held the twig thoughtfully for a few seconds as if meditating on the larger meaning of life and all that it held in store for them, then passed it on delicately as if overwhelmed by what they had considered about life.

Elizabeth bent and scooped up a handful of dirt then stood and let the dirt trickle through her open fingers. Ah ha, thought Rayanne, borrowed from the Catholic burial rites. Elizabeth said, "This is earth. All life comes from the earth."

Elizabeth brushed the dirt out of her hand and dug into her pockets again, coming out with a vial of liquid.

Holy water? Rayanne wondered.

"Water from the creek that runs beside my door," said Elizabeth. "Water is what preserves life." She opened the small jar and wet her finger which she touched to Montana's cheeks, first one then the other. "Water will sustain you. Water is the blood of life."

This must be a twist on the rite of communion, a twist that Rayanne had never heard before.

Replacing the water jar in her dress, Elizabeth led Karla and Montana into the direct sunlight.

"The sun," she said as the baby blinked fiercely. "All life comes from the sun."

Then turning to all the others she said, "Wood, earth, water and sun. These are the four corners of life. In life we are one."

She turned to the baby, "Welcome to life, Montana Louise. Welcome to oneness with all people, with all living things. Let us go now and celebrate."

How do Druids celebrate, Rayanne wondered. Are we all going to dance naked through the woods?

＊   ＊   ＊   ＊

Celebrating, it turned out, consisted of ice cream for the children with wine and coffee for the adults. Karla asked for herbal tea. Some of Karla's entourage—midwife, assistants and the pregnant observer—asked for herbal tea also. A bit guiltily, it seemed to Rayanne, who was already thinking about having a second glass of white wine after she finished this one. The bottle was marked as a Virginia wine, labeled with a picture that resembled the front gate where they had turned in this morning.

Their hostess's name, Rayanne discovered, was Rosemary, and she hung around the old woman, as if she, Elizabeth, really were a celebrity.

Noor, who had been clicking away during the ceremony, was everywhere now, a thin figure in black, a part of the background, trying various angles, up, down, straight on, recording everything that interested her. Rayanne wished she were at home in bed, with a good book. Another glass of this wine might not be so bad, though.

*   *   *   *

Maybe she had had too many glasses of wine. Rayanne couldn't remember how many, but as her head began to clear on the drive back to Alexandria she recollected several things. Someone said that the old woman was a crone. Someone else explained that "crone" was another way of saying "wise woman," more of a title than an actual description of a person.

Being a crone was very important to these people. She hadn't previously thought of them as being "these people" as if they had anything particular in common other than a very low key way of wasting a perfectly good Saturday.

Also she foggily remembered that the hostess, Rosemary, wanted a painted portrait of the crone, and that she and Noor had promised to visit the old woman next week. Noor would take pictures that would give Rayanne the setting she wanted and some photographs of Elizabeth from various angles that she would use for assembling the portrait back in her studio.

On sober reflection, and she *was* gradually sobering and reflecting, this was probably the dumbest thing she'd ever agreed to do. Shit.

CHAPTER 24

▼

ELIZABETH'S

Awe was not a familiar sensation for Rayanne, but awe was what she felt, staring at Elizabeth's house from the front seat of Noor's Jeep. It was an old Virginia farm house, one story high, with a sagging front porch and a sway-backed roof to match. The whole place, front yard, fences, and outbuildings, projected not so much a neglected look as a forgotten look. It was as if the original owners had suddenly taken a notion to try farming and, after constructing a few buildings, took a notion just as suddenly to walk away and leave farming forever, and everything connected with it.

The place was unbelievably isolated, to Rayanne's way of looking at things. It was not on a highway. Neither was it on a secondary road off a highway. She had lost count, but it seemed to her that the road that terminated at Elizabeth's front gate was the fifth or sixth generation of successively more decrepit byways. Over the last few roads the track had degenerated from pavement to gravel, then to dirt, then to ruts and now to little more than twin tracks through a field.

She was not glad to be here. "Relieved" was too elevated an emotion for what she felt. In her mind she could see a title for an oil painting, "Desolation in Hunt Country," but for once she could visualize no image to go with it. No image except this, this haphazard collection of architectural disappointments in the weeds in front of her.

"We're here," said Noor unnecessarily, and opened the driver's side door. Rayanne reluctantly opened the passenger side door and got out.

She saw Noor hesitate over picking up her camera bag and tripod, then noticed Noor shake her head and turn away, leaving her gear in the car. Noor would be thinking this might not be the place, so she would wait before unloading all her stuff.

They walked up onto the porch together. Noor knocked. Rayanne cringed.

"You the painters?" A man came from around the porch from the side yard. He was relatively young, Rayanne guessed late thirties. Maybe Elizabeth's son.

"She's a painter," answered Noor, stepping down into the yard. "I'm the photographer." This title was delivered with a certain emphasis as if the photographer's class outranked the painter's class.

"We're both artists, really," Rayanne offered to the man, hoping she didn't sound defensive or argumentative, and realizing she sounded *both* defensive *and* argumentative. This day was not going well already.

He held out his hand. "I'm Elizabeth's husband." His smile flashed even before the disbelief registered on their faces. "Yes, I'm forty-three."

He waited, as if listening for the beat. "And, yes, Elizabeth's eighty."

Another beat. "I get that all the time."

"How about that?" said Noor.

His smile was unchanged. It sat on his face as if we were a public relations official. "My name is Ferlin Mayo."

Rayanne gave their names.

"Yes, Elizabeth told me. Come on in. She's expecting you."

Damn right, Rayanne thought to herself. Almost two hours' drive out of town, she'd sure as hell better be expecting us.

Beneath that voice in her head she heard another voice asking why she let Noor drag her to all these God forsaken places. One of these days she was going to have to learn to drive. Or, more accurately, learn the way other people drive, how to stop at stop signs, how to stay on the right side of the road, and how to get where you're going without hitting another car or killing somebody.

Noor collected her stuff.

The man opened the screen door for them and followed them into the hall. After the bright light of the summer outdoors the hall was dark and crowded with things you might bump into and break. Acres of whatnots. Little glass things, like horses and snowmen and upside down cups and starfish. Interspersed among all the glass things were tiny wreaths and crosses made of twigs and straw.

There were more stick crosses and bundles of twigs over the doorways off to either side of the hall, she saw as her eyes adjusted to the absence of light. It was brighter off to the left and they turned that way into a wide, low-ceilinged room that turned out to be a combination living room, dining room and kitchen.

Rayanne wondered what all the other rooms were for. When she saw that the kitchen included a day bed she decided the other rooms must be abandoned, then she caught herself wondering where the man slept, since the daybed was obviously only a twin bed. Then she wondered why the young man would want to share a bed with the older woman anyway. Then she told herself to shut up and stop wondering. Then she wondered how you could paint the idea of not wondering. Then she told herself to shut up, shut up, shut up. Then she did.

CHAPTER 25

▼

SHOOT

The kitchen was hot, too hot. Even so the old woman, Elizabeth, was wearing a sweater. She sat at a large table that occupied most of an alcove to the side of the cooking area. The space where she sat had windows on two sides. There were newspapers and the remnants of knitting and what appeared to be a pile of bills on the table. This had to be Elizabeth's center of operations. She did not get up when they came in.

"How was your drive?" She smiled at them. Rayanne thought there was too much smiling going on for so early in the morning.

"Fine," said Noor.

"Long," said Rayanne, then embarrassed at being so candid she added a half-laugh. Elizabeth's smile lay unchanged on her face.

"Then you'll want some tea," said Elizabeth. "Ferlin can get it for you."

"Coffee, if you have it," said Noor. Impulsiveness and honesty were two things about Noor that Rayanne really couldn't stand, especially before noon. She tried to give Noor a tea-is-what-they-offer-tea-is-what-you-take kind of look but it went right over Noor's head.

"We have instant. Is that okay?" the man said. He looked improbably young to be this woman's husband. Rayanne felt there was some exquisitely balanced pile of needs here. A tensely balanced foundation that she just needed to find the right chink to poke at and it would all come tumbling down.

"Tea with milk and sugar would suit me," she said. That was not the linchpin. Nothing fell.

"Sure," he said, the smile firmly in place. "And there's hot water so the coffee will be good to go."

Rayanne hated the expression "good to go." It was one of those sayings like "have a nice day" that had crept into everyday conversations when she wasn't looking. She vowed once again to get a television some day and actually watch it.

Her personal theory was that certain phrases periodically swept the country from some broadcasting center in Chicago, like an aura spreading out, or the stink of manure. She'd paint that, too, after her TV experiment was finished. She figured she would be good for, oh, maybe three days of concentrated watching. Her stomach heaved at the thought and her throat constricted. She really needed some caffeine.

"Here you go," said Ferlin. He handed Noor a cup of steaming coffee, black, glowing with the hot smell of caffeine. The cup he placed in Rayanne's eager hands turned out to be filled with a thin, insipid liquid that was as much clear as it was brown.

"Virginia herbs. Local herbs from Elizabeth's garden," he said, responding to Rayanne's fuddled look. In Rayanne's head "local herbs" translated into "no caffeine." She formed the word "shit" mentally and forced herself not to share the feeling with all these smiling people.

Noor was busy looking around the room for background-type stuff and asking if she could move this and that, ooh-ing and ah-ing about the light and asking Elizabeth to turn her head this way and that.

Rayanne found herself standing beside the still-smiling man. It seemed like the time to say something friendly. What did friendly people talk about before noon? "A little warm in here, isn't it?"

"Elizabeth's cold-natured," he said. "We're both cold-natured." His smile seemed to weaken, then firmed up. Rayanne noticed he was wearing long sleeves in all this heat. Rayanne was wearing her usual sleeveless shift. She wondered what Ferlin would look like without his shirt. He seemed thin. She pictured him with abs and wondered if he would like to pose.

Something about her face must have changed. His smile faded and he said, "I got chores." Then, to Elizabeth, "Will you be all right?"

Elizabeth nodded without taking her eyes from Noor who was busily rearranging the skeins of yarn on the table. Noor had already carried the newspapers and bills off to a side table.

Typhoon Noor—Rayanne had a sense of the storm that was Noor attacking her life, strewing wreckage all about, and for a moment she sympathized with the vulnerability that Elizabeth must be feeling. A look at the serene expression on Elizabeth's face, however, convinced Rayanne that her sympathies were misplaced. No one was going to derail this woman. There were three women in this room. Three women in this house, but one woman only was in charge and that woman was clearly Elizabeth. That woman would always be Elizabeth. There was a sense of power in the room and it did not come from either of the artists. Elizabeth would be running the show, no doubt about it.

Noor had her tripod out now and was asking Elizabeth to turn this way and that, put her chin on her hands, lean her elbows on the table, gather her scarf up around her neck, and on and on. The camera clicked now and again. It might have seemed that Noor was calling the shots, but Elizabeth had surprisingly expressive eyes and she managed to telegraph to the artists which poses she liked and which she considered bad ideas.

Every time the "bad idea" flag registered Noor would immediately call out, "Umm, no, how about this instead?"

To Rayanne's critical eye Noor and Elizabeth were puppet and puppeteer and she marveled that Noor didn't sense the connection. She felt a painting materializing in her mind and she was not happy with the image. It was heavy with reds and blacks, a large hand in the foreground with strings bow-tied at the finger tips and converging on a distant figure, visible as a tiny head and shoulders.

She tried to switch off the image but she knew from sad experience it would always be there in her mental to-be-painted file. It might some day rise up and possess her till she rendered it tactile on canvas, her way of choking the life out of each particular demon and cleansing her burning head.

"Dear, would you like to sit down?" Of course Elizabeth had picked up on Rayanne's discomfort. She might have been a manipulator, but at least she wasn't insensitive.

"No, thanks, I'm not tired, just restless," said Rayanne.

"Why don't you look around, then?" Here it came, the manipulation. "There are some interesting old things here," continued the puppeteer's voice. "They belonged to my mother. Some of them came from my grandmother."

"I'd love to," Rayanne tried on her sweet voice. It seemed to fit, maybe the tea had a little kick to it after all. "If you don't mind."

"You go right ahead, dear."

Rayanne hated being called dear, almost as much as she hated being called little lady. She gathered up her fortitude and went out to prowl the kitchen.

There was practically nothing electronic and very little that was even electric in the kitchen. How could they make espresso, she wondered, or even toast a bagel? The gas stove had a familiar, if superannuated, sort of look, but the wood stove baffled her completely. She would not even have realized what it was if not for the pile of split wood stacked up behind it.

The kitchen, like the hall before it, was decorated with ceramic figures, glass figurines and little bits of twigs twisted and shaped into circles and crosses. Here and there were rocks of all sizes, some as big as eggs, some as tiny as jelly beans, with shiny particles like crystal reflecting out of them. She had seen decorations like these recently, but could not remember where.

CHAPTER 26

▼

CHICKENS

Rayanne walked back into the dining area. Noor now had Elizabeth standing. Rayanne nodded inwardly, admiring how Noor had found a way to bounce light off the newspaper and counterbalance the shadow from the eaves outside the window that would have obscured Elizabeth's face.

"Did you find anything interesting, dear?"

"It was all lovely," said Rayanne, mustering a gracious tone. Now I know there's something in the tea, she thought.

"I have reached the stage in my life where I have started to give my things away," said Elizabeth. "If you see something you would really like to have, let me know."

She hadn't actually said "I'll give it to you," Rayanne realized. This woman is a crafty politician. She's getting credit for being generous without actually parting with a thing. Wonder if I'll be like that when I'm her age.

Elizabeth had already turned back to Noor. "Would you like to do some pictures outside?"

"Would you mind?" asked Noor.

"My goodness, no. I love the out-of-doors. I was raised a farm girl. Let me just get my wrap."

Outside Noor worked faster. She photographed Elizabeth in her apple orchard, much the same way as she had done the christening pictures, with dappled light falling first this way then another on Elizabeth's wrinkled face and shoulders. Rayanne thought about how she would alternately mute and brighten the colors when she was painting and began to warm up to Noor's intuitions.

There was a pond some distance out behind the house and orchard. Noor posed Elizabeth down at the pond with her head raised, looking over to where Noor and her tripod stood some several feet away, giving an impression of solitary wistfulness that Rayanne could already envision on canvas.

The three of them walked back up the hill toward the house then veered off to an old greyish building that Elizabeth said was the chicken coop. Rayanne could tell that Noor was thrilling to the feel of the weathered boards that covered the sides of the building. They were fastened vertically with a texture that could not help but be visually exciting in large prints.

Rayanne could already imagine the big 16 x 20 portraits that Noor must be mentally salivating over. She knew that Noor would print them in black and white. This was first class gallery material in a mawkish Dorothea Lange sort of way, but it was the kind of thing that the independent dealers got all mushy over. They were guaranteed sells to a sentimental and unsophisticated buying public.

She could imagine currency flowing into Noor's hands after all of this had fallen into her lap. Rayanne, on the other hand, would be lucky to collect her fee for the one painting of this woman that she had been commissioned to produce. Life, Rayanne was beginning to suspect again, maybe for the millionth time, was not fair.

Out here in the silence the shutter clicked once more.

"Could we stop for now?" Elizabeth asked, in a tone of voice that Rayanne thought surely mean, not "for now" but "for good."

"Yeah, sure, whatever," said Noor.

Whatever, sniffed Rayanne, mentally. Today was just going to be one of those days when all the trite expressions that had sneaked up on her while she wasn't looking were going to get trotted out by people she couldn't avoid.

"There's a pullet I've been meaning to cook for dinner," Elizabeth said. She opened the wire gate into the hen yard next to the building. "If you want to come in you might just pick up one of those sticks by the side there to defend yourself. I have a flogging rooster and if you don't watch yourself he's likely to sneak up behind and flog you a good one."

They both hung back.

Elizabeth closed the chicken wire gate behind her. Calling "He-e-ere, chick, chick, chick, he-e-ere, chick, chick, chick," she walked slowly over to a bunch of chickens crowding ahead of her into one corner. So quickly they almost missed it she reached in and grabbed one.

Emerging from the enclosure with the chicken caught fast in her arms she warned them to stand aside. Then to their astonishment she took the chicken by the neck with one hand and released the other one. Then, with a gesture surprising in its strength she whirled the chicken around in the air, like a kid throwing half of a very fast jump rope. Suddenly there was a snap of her wrist, almost faster than they could follow, and the body of the chicken went flying off and hit the side of the building, its head still clutched in her hand.

The headless body bounced down onto the ground, landing on its tail. It jerked up. It flopped around the yard, legs kicking together. The body lunged forward then sideways, blood spurting out of its open neck. It bounced all over the yard. It fell to the ground jerking spasmodically and kicking. Elizabeth watched the wretched blood-splattered body emotionlessly then, without looking at it, tossed the head that was still in her hand, back into the chicken yard where the other chickens immediately ran at it, pecking it to pieces.

CHAPTER 27

▼

ECHO

Noor watched the whole performance in fascination. Rayanne had never felt so sick.

In the car, on the way home, she made Noor pull over so she could get out of the car. She needed the rush of cold air in her face. It was hard to believe that on such a hot day the air could feel so cool against her skin. The air conditioning inside the car had been no help at all. Out here she could feel open again, opened up and clean. She hated the thought of getting back inside the car and letting the door close behind her. Hated it, but did it. Twice.

At last she was in control of herself, this self with the fragile trembling body. It was like being in the middle of a particularly nasty bout with the flu.

Noor looked at her with something like disgust. Maybe not disgust exactly, but something very like an expression of emotional superiority. "Okay, what's the matter?"

And, after a while, "Let's get it all out, Rayanne."

Rayanne sniffled. She was a little girl again, well, maybe not but, you know, it would have felt really good just then to have a shoulder somewhere, a big, warm, strong shoulder to rest her head on. But not Noor's.

"I don't know," she said. "No, yes I do. Didn't you notice, how she was with the chicken? She didn't feel sorry for that chicken at all. Not one bit."

"Feel sorry, Rayanne? For a chicken?"

"Well … yes. A chicken." What was the matter with this world? Didn't anyone care about anything any more? Didn't anybody know what sympathy was any more? How did you tell someone what she was supposed to feel? Where had their mothers been all their lives? Is this what a cultural gap was?

A paradigm shift. That was what she needed. She had to give Noor a paradigm shift. Let her know what she was supposed to feel. Let everybody know. That was it. That was what the whole word needed, a paradigm shift. The whole world. The whole goddamned world.

"Rayanne."

"Hmm?"

"Rayanne?"

"What?"

"You're drifting."

"Drifting?"

"Is there an echo in here?"

"Noor, what are you talking about?"

"I'm talking about what's the matter with you."

"There's nothing the matter with me."

"I know you, Rayanne. You're off somewhere and it's starting to bug me."

Rayanne felt the resentment and the hurt begin to build up inside her. Wasn't Noor her friend?

"You're off again, Rayanne. I can feel it. It's something about that woman. Yes, that's what it is. So, come on, out with it."

Why did Noor treat her sometimes like she was just a little girl? She was always acting like Rayanne's big sister. Or big brother. She wished Noor would decide which side of the fence she lived on. It would make everything so much easier.

"Rayanne?"

"What?"

"You're doing it again."

"Doing what?"

"There's that echo again, god damn it. I'm going to stop the car."

"Good, 'cause I'm about to puke."

This time when she got back into the car her head was clearer.

"I thought about it."

"Good."

"It's about Elizabeth."

"I knew it."

"It's about the way she killed that chicken."

"God damn. Not the chicken again."

"Will you listen to me a minute?"

"I'll shut up."

"I don't mean that … yes, I do. See, if it was you or me that did it, we'd look different."

"I certainly hope so. She's old enough to be our grandmother."

"I don't mean that. Are you going to hear me out or not?"

"Right."

What did 'right' mean? Rayanne didn't know but this time she wasn't going to stop and think about it. She hated it when Noor picked on her. It only made it feel like Noor was reading her mind and it always made her feel inferior. How could you have a best friend that made you feel inferior? If she was your best friend wouldn't you be equals? Whoops, there she was going again and Noor was getting that puckering up look, like she was going to say something. Rayanne rushed on, as if trying to catch up with herself.

"Let me tell you, let me say this. I'm trying to let you know what I was feeling. Maybe you didn't feel the same thing." Noor was getting that of-course-not-are-you-crazy kind of look. Rayanne hurried ahead.

"See, when I was little I killed something. A parakeet."

"You're kidding."

"Well, I did … no, I didn't."

"Rayanne!" That was it. That tone of exasperation. That you've-done-it-now-that's-the-end-of-our-friendship look. It was on Noor's face and the next minute she was going to say it and Rayanne would just die. Right there in the front seat of the car. Sixty miles an hour on the highway into D.C. and her body dead in the front seat. She wanted to take a minute and arrange all the characters and the props like a scene in a play and think about the lighting and the style of clothes and the period furniture but she saw a word forming on Noor's lips that was beginning to resemble the first stages of the f-word and she had to rush on.

"What I'm trying to say is that I may have been too young to do what I thought I did. There were these two kittens in Oklahoma. Maybe I killed them, too."

Rayanne watched with anxious eyes as Noor, staring ahead into the traffic, let out a long breath with an audible whoosh. Then she told Noor about the manuscript she had found in a box the year after her dad moved out.

CHAPTER 28

▼

KILLING WAY

A Story
by Ronald Tellsworth

It was something about the way rats had of running. A rat runs low and silent, legs nearly hidden beneath its body, its naked obscene tail sliding cowardly behind. It was something about the arrogance of it, how they moved. Even in the daylight. Shouldering close along the wall, where the wall met the ground, where the falling rain threw up the gravel and kept the grass from growing, in the shade of clapboards and broken things.

As a boy he had killed a mouse, or so he remembered. His family were poor and, like many city poor, ignorant of tools. What tools they had, had many purposes. They kept their flour in a flour bin that fitted loosely into a broad lower compartment of the kitchen cupboard. Where it swung down to allow you to dip a cup. Where you didn't dare open it to look inside unless you were told to get some flour. The compartment was lined with tin, and the flour floated lazily up into the air if you so much as opened a crack.

His mother found a mouse in there one day and slammed the door on its soft grey underbelly. Its head stuck out and thrashed about frantically. "Kill it," she had ordered him and handed him a broom. He knocked at the tiny head with its two black eyes. Knocked again and again at the nose jerking up into the sky as if drowning. Knocked at it till finally blood ran out of the tiny nostrils, and the head went limp, and he could pick up the soft warm body with newspapers and put it out into the garbage. The garbage can was a hot, fetid thing in the summer air with swarms of startled, bloated white maggots writhing inside when the lid came up.

As a boy he had killed a mouse, at least he thought he had killed it. But he didn't think you could kill a rat.

*   *   *   *

A rat was a perverse, dirty thing that bit little children who slept on the floor. But a mouse could maybe be a good thing. His classmate's father had caught a whistling mouse once. Kept it in a cage till the newspaper came and wrote a story about it, and Roscoe said they could hear it whistling at night while they were all in bed. His classmates called Roscoe by the nickname Sonny, but the boy who killed the mouse didn't know that, and he got the names mixed up and thought for months that Roscoe was the name of Sonny's whistling mouse.

Sonny dropped out of school in the eighth grade, and the boy who killed the mouse had forgotten about him till he appeared one day outside the open high school window, hollering over the sound of the teacher's voice for a boy named Jerry to throw him the keys to the delivery truck. Sonny had gotten a job working for Jerry's father during the hours while Jerry was in school studying.

This Jerry was the class clown, who was impossibly the heartthrob of the school cellist and who went on to become a Doctor of medieval English literature. The cellist raised two sons and gave a reading of a feminist paper in favor of women priests when the Pope came to visit. The Pope thanked her and asked her to sit down.

*   *   *   *

Being poor they killed their own chickens. His mother could do it but his father was best at it. He'd take the bird by its head and spin it round and round in his hand, wringing its neck till the body flew off, bounced against the garage wall, and flopped to the ground. It would jump around bleeding through the stump between its feathers till at last the headless body fell over, legs kicking out at the grass. Sometimes there might be two chickens, especially on a Sunday, because his father, who was a big man, liked a big Sunday dinner. Usually they were Rhode Island Reds.

Having a backyard to kill chickens was actually a step up, because you got to go inside to the bathroom afterwards to wash up. Before that they had lived in a place that was not quite country and not quite town, a little place with a hydrant out in the front yard where you went for water. Its nozzle was turned upwards so you could drink out of it when you weren't filling a pail. You had to run the faucet a while before the water turned cold and good to drink.

The bathroom was a two-hole outhouse that you got to by walking through the chicken yard. If you were a little child you carried a stick, like a short beanpole, in case the rooster tried to flog you. The kinds of chickens his dad killed were Rhode Island Reds. He had never seen his father kill a Dominecker. Domineckers were more agreeable and they laid the most eggs. But the rooster was a Rhode Island Red. Rhode Island Reds make the best roosters.

*   *   *   *

Once a classmate's father gave the boy two pigeons. There was an epidemic of ringworm that year and to the boy who killed the mouse it felt deliciously daring to visit his classmate's house where the two boys of the family had to wear stockings over their shaved heads because of the ringworms. He was proud of the pigeons he came home with and his mother named them "Patrick" and "Patricia."

His father fastened a wire door to a ramshackle outbuilding with palings warped and rotted. The father built a shoebox sized wooden nest on a crossbeam and the boy filled it with straw. Through the wire mesh door the boy saw the female go to the box. The male flew close up beside her and turned circles cooing throatily in the way of pigeons. After a few days the boy saw that the female no longer bobbed her head nervously in the nest when he came to feed them. Surprised at his own boldness he reached up to her in the straw and found nothing but a backside and tail feathers. Rats had eaten away her entire underbody. There were no eggs in the nest.

The ringworm boy took chemical engineering and made himself into an oil company executive too busy to attend their class reunion. The executive's mother had smoked always and died early of cancer in the lungs.

*   *   *   *

When the boy who killed the mouse ran away from home for a time, he wanted very much to believe he had gotten chased off, but in fact his father would have been happy to keep him around for the fun of beating up on him. The truth was he had feared more the humiliation of the beatings in front of his friends and had run away to avoid the shame. His sisters took the blows. The father died, the boy grew up. The boy's friends pitied him because his father died, and the boy who killed the mouse wondered how their minds had frozen like mastodons in ice without understanding what the father had been like to the son.

There was less killing but, after he learned to drive and to notice things, he came to wonder what happened to the cats and dogs run over. Who picked up the carcasses or dragged them off to the trash? In later years he came to realize that vultures and crows and beetles came when your back was turned—small wonder that people believed in spirits and things that made no reflections in mirrors.

*   *   *   *

His mother kept a parakeet that in his senior high school year developed an affliction. Its appetite fell off. Its eyes got rimmed with white scales, one leg drew up, and a wing dragged. Eventually it could not keep itself upright and would flop jerkily about the floor of its cage, rustling spastically among the torn sheets of newspaper. "I want you to kill it," his mother told him, and she went outdoors.

Even in his high school years they were poor. There were no tools, and the boy who had killed the mouse took a paring knife to the neck of the parakeet among the blue green feathers and heard the bones crackle as the knife bit through. It was not a sharp knife. Poor people had to make do as much out of lack of knowledge as out of a surplus of want, and his one grandfather who had an emery wheel for sharpening knives was an hour's drive away and there was neither gas for the car nor permission to drive. Ultimately the bird died of the weight of the boy's body pushing the knife through its neckbones, more crushed than sliced.

The mother threw away the parakeet's cage. Later she raised a Pomeranian dog when her daughter went away, first off to school and then to marriage. In its first year the dog lost an eye. Pomeranians have a popeyed look anyway. Some call it bug-eyed. She kept the dog till it died, sweeping up its shed hairs, and bringing it in from the summer heat. It died right after she bought herself a room air conditioner.

*   *   *   *

In adulthood, between wives and alone in a subdivided ante-bellum apartment with wide plank floors and cracks so broad he could see between the joists, over a period of several nights he woke to a coarse wood-cutting sound, like a big-toothed saw drawn over dry kindling. Slow, steady, deliberate, it would persist for fifteen or twenty minutes then stop. Lying in bed he could not make out just where the cutting sound came from. One night, reading in his kitchen, he heard it again. From an unused cupboard, and just behind him. He rose on tiptoe and jerked open the cupboard door.

In the wall at the back of the cupboard, about eye level, he saw an irregular hole, about the size of a half dollar, just big enough for the triangular black shape inside it, the underside of the upper end of the head of a rat, long teeth showing, a pointed nose above, and a black eye peering sideways. A malevolent, unblinking eye.

He slammed the door, and listened for it to panic and fall back down between the walls. But there was no sound. No movement. That night he slept poorly. Next day he nailed the top of a soup can over the opening in the wall. The cabinet had been bone-empty. The cabinet could not possibly have smelled of food for all the desiccation of its years standing empty. Still, it bothered him, what the rat was after.

✳   ✳   ✳   ✳

He told all of these things to the man beside him on the concrete stoop. The sun was hot coming after the morning's rain, and he could feel it on his knees. Soon someone would come from inside and move him back further into the shade, and out of the sun. If they didn't forget. Lately he had begun to worry if they would remember.

He was pleased today that his roommate felt like talking, he hoped it would last. He had done his best to entertain the old man, remembering to laugh out loud in all the funny parts, to speed up in the beginnings and to talk a little slower at the ends. Now the boy who had killed the mouse turned, as best he could, to look at his companion.

The old man was asleep, his head fallen against the cloth tied round the wings of his wheeled chair. Past the old man, in the narrow trench alongside the building where the raindrops still dripped from the roof, the boy, now old, who had once killed a mouse, saw a dark movement. A rat ran along in the slight hollow, deliberate and intent, its feet scarcely visible, trailing a thin naked tail.

CHAPTER 29

▼

DAD

Ronnie Tellsworth's full name was Ronald Tyndahl Tellsworth. Both Rayanne and her father were listed in the Northern Virginia phonebook as R. T. Tellsworth, because Rayanne's middle name was Taylor, her mother's family name. This meant that Rayanne often got her dad's phone calls, which more often than not were from women, since he had been single most of Rayanne's life.

They also had the same zip code which meant Rayanne received lots of her dad's mail which she scrupulously avoided reading, except for the magazine titles and illustrated envelopes which she could not avoid seeing. He seemed to get, she felt, more than his fair share of senior citizen life enhancement material, focusing too much, she thought, on aphrodisiacs and gray-haired couples on sunset beaches.

Most of the handwritten first class mail that came to her in beautiful penmanship she knew without looking must be for her dad since none of her acquaintances had wasted any self-discipline on small muscle control exercises. Still, if the handwriting or the return address was unfamiliar, she was forced to open the envelope, just to make certain that the letter was not for her.

Well! She was forever amazed at how aggressive, and explicit, her dad's various new women acquaintances could be—in writing.

She had occasionally been introduced to one of Ronnie's girlfriends after she had accidentally opened and read one of the woman's letters and she was always shocked by the difference between the person she expected and the person she met. What she actually saw in the flesh was someone's charming, exquisitely toned, expensively dressed, older sister.

Mostly they were petite. Her dad preferred women shorter than he was, and he himself was barely five foot six inches tall. His women friends tended to be gushy and twittery, laughing softly and musically in the upper registers. Being with them for awhile was like marching in the back of the percussion section of a school band in the midst of the triangles and the lyre players.

That Ronnie Tellsworth hooked these clinging vines and shrinking violets amazed Rayanne, ever and again. It had to be the square jaw that she had inherited, more exaggerated in him. It gave him a certain masculine, almost macho, look that, when taken with his weight lifting muscles and his tennis energy, gave him a certain atmosphere of competent ruggedness. Rayanne knew better. Way, way better.

If anything, the kind of woman Ronnie Tellsworth needed was exactly the kind he had married and with whom he had begotten Rayanne. A strong, take-charge, hard working, no nonsense farm girl, Wanda Joyce Taylor, from central Illinois whom he had met on shore leave in Chicago.

He was fresh out of the Academy, a Navy pilot. Wanda had been visiting a friend, her first outing from Golconda, Illinois, since high school graduation three years earlier.

Wanda and Ronnie had been exactly the same height, very convenient for kissing in the day time, but a pain in the neck when she wore heels on a date. In fact, Rayanne's mother used to say, "Ronnie and I never would have gotten engaged if I hadn't borrowed Jeanne's car." Jeanne was the friend she'd been visiting in Chicago. Their courtship had been conducted sitting down. For the most part.

Their love had been mutually satisfactory, Rayanne had learned, but if one of them had fared better in the match it had been her dad. Ronald Tellsworth had needed a woman who would manage him and his life the way a combination White House Chief of Staff, valet and personal physician would manage the President of the United States, controlling where he went and whom he met, seeing to his wardrobe and his diet, remembering his birthday and anniversary obligations and raising his daughter.

After Ronnie made captain, whenever he received any assignment where spouses were welcome, like his tour as base commandant at the Naval Weapons Lab in Dahlgren, Virginia, Wanda Joyce had gone along as unofficial second-in-command and—his people skills being what they were, effectively nil—

seen that he succeeded by pushing him everywhere he needed to be, and when, and told him what to say when he got there.

Wanda Joyce had died when Rayanne was twelve years old. Her mom and dad had been married twenty years. Ronnie turned ineffectual in his next assignment and, with the encouragement of his closest remaining mentor, opted to take the retirement he had earned and vacate the Service. If he had stayed in, hoping for promotion to admiral, the country would have had to go to war—and into a war so resource hungry that Congress would have blindly elevated everyone with seniority—for Ronnie to have had at best an even odds shot at promotion to flag officer.

Since retirement Ronnie had depended on his "ring knocker" connections from Academy days for a succession of consultant's jobs that kept him in poolside condos and elevator shoes. He developed a certain fondness for chorus line show-girls and backup singers in rock bands, and, to his own surprise, cultivated a sure instinct for the inexperienced and the naive. Seldom was he disappointed in their interest in sharing a good time. Seldom were his expenses more than he could easily afford. It was as if he could smell the "coq-au-vin at my place" ingredients on their fingertips while they were getting introduced.

Usually the letters or the phone calls that Rayanne received came after the first or second date. By the fourth or fifth date the woman and Ronnie himself had lost interest and gone on to more promising partnerships. Why, Rayanne kept asking herself, why do they keep falling for this guy? What attracted women to her dad had to be his rugged square jawed looks, like a combination between Alexander Haig and Telly Savalis. Maybe they mistook his baldness for a crewcut?

Despite all his shortcomings, now, at this moment, she felt that she really needed her dad. She would like to go to him, to simply sit down with him and tell him all that bothered her, this business of Elba and Elba's dying, and every-body else's dying.

She wished it could be her father's house where she could visit, where she could unload, just let her shoes slide off her feet and lean back in a chair on his deck, two stories above the ground where it jutted out over the former swamp that now formed the shores of the Potomac River.

Her dad's condo was just a mile or so south of her, along the George Wash-ington Parkway, on the way to Mount Vernon, where the river ran along close to the road and it was all rushes and reeds and tidal coves snuggling up to high, rounded, lawn-covered banks.

To just lean back and have him massage her neck the way he used to when she first started putting in the long days at the easel. And to talk just loud enough for him to hear behind her while her eyes closed and the images in the shadows of her vision gradually burned away and were replaced by green living things and blue skies and looser, brighter shadows.

To just hear herself rambling on, the way she used to in her dreaming moods, as if all the things that had hurt her today had happened to somebody else, as if all those horrible things had gradually faded further and further away, somewhere into a land of myth and make believe.

She wanted to tell him things that were just for his ears only. But she could not go to his condo, could not wander through the den where some of his books were shelved, the spare bedroom that had been converted to a library where more of his books were stacked and arranged, and where there was a rollaway bed in a closet for her, and into his own bedroom, military straight, where other books lay on dressers and chests and on the floor.

She would like to, but she could not.

Because they would not be alone.

Whoever he was seeing would be there. Maybe not in the flesh. Especially not in the evenings. Not if she were an entertainer, working at night. Not in the actual flesh. The actual, paintable, drawable flesh. But her presence would be there. A woman's shoe beside the closet door, suggesting its mate would be inside if you opened the closet. Lipstick, deodorant in the bathroom. Some of his women friends used the same scents, maybe that's what attracted him to them. But never the same color lipstick. Why? Never the same hair color, two women in a row. Again why?

Whoever the lady of the moment might be, the effect of her presence would declare itself. Rayanne could imagine a picture propped against the lamp on his side of the bed, the left side, where Rayanne's mother's picture had stood during the first few years after her death. It had stayed there through the early succession of Ronnie Tellsworth's girlfriends, but had not survived one particularly tempestuous affair where the glass had gotten itself broken and never managed to get itself replaced.

She hoped he still had the picture. It was her favorite of her mother. It had been taken of her mother in the 60's, wearing a granny dress just like Rayanne favored today, thick-soled square-toed shoes, sitting on a concrete ledge in some big town, maybe San Francisco, head tilted back, arms flung out to either side along the wall behind her, knees turned out, deeply cut bodice showing the topography of a chest clearly unfettered by any bra, glad and sassy, turning her eyes to the camera.

CHAPTER 30

▼

AFTER ELIZABETH'S

"Noor, I think now that I didn't kill that parakeet after all." They were in Rayanne's studio-apartment. She was looking at Noor and absent-mindedly scratching Señor Cee's brindle head.

"Good. Let's drop it then. Time for me to split."

"No. Listen. What I think now is that I killed the kittens." She jerked her hand away from Señor Cee's head as she said it.

"Rayanne, I am out of here."

"No! Listen to me. Just listen!"

"For God's sake, Rayanne. What makes you think I care about kittens?"

"It's not about kittens. It's about killing. I'm talking about what it's like to kill something."

"People kill things all the time, Rayanne. Sometimes it's a mosquito that lands on your arm. Sometimes it's a polecat you hit with your car."

"Noor, do you care about anything at all?"

"Yes, I do care, but not about kittens."

"About killing. Killing! *Killing! Listen to me!!*"

"O. K.," quietly. Nora gave a shrug.

"I was five years old. Daddy was in service. He was stationed in Oklahoma. We went to stay with him. My sister went with us. She was two years younger than me."

"I didn't know you had a sister, Rayanne."

"Shut up, Noor."

"O.K.," quietly, for once.

"I had been sick. I think I had been sick. We were in the back yard. Only it wasn't a yard. It was all sand. Nothing but sand. And a concrete sidewalk, or something like that, in the back yard. Ant hills, too. I know now that there were ant hills, but I didn't know it then. We played outside. Once I went running in and I was scared and there were ants all over me. Mother took all my clothes off. She rubbed me with coal oil. There were ants everywhere. There were ants on my, in my ..."

"I don't want to hear this, Rayanne." Noor's voice had grown firm. Very firm. Teeth-gritting firm.

"I meant to tell you about the kittens. Let me just tell you about the baby cats."

"Is this going to get us anywhere?"

"Yes, Noor. Just listen to me."

"O.K.," resignedly.

"I think there was a mother cat. I don't really remember her."

"All right."

"She had two kittens. They were yellow."

"Only two?"

"That's all I remember."

"Is that it?"

"No. I'm trying to tell you."

No response.

"There was something about me being sick. Something about cats carrying ringworms. I think my mother was afraid of them. I remember myself swinging them by their tails, like a windmill. No, like John Henry swinging his hammers. I remember hitting their heads on the sidewalk where it stuck out. Bang, one head, then bang, the other head."

"Rayanne!"

"When I was grown I said something to my mother about killing the little cats. She said it never happened."

"Well, she would know, wouldn't she? How would a five-year old kid have the strength to swing kittens in the air by their tails and hit their heads on a sidewalk?"

"That's what I thought, Noor, but I can still see them lying on the sand, blood running out of their noses."

"Rayanne, your mother would know. She would know."

"Maybe so, maybe not. Maybe she only told me it didn't happen, just to protect my mind. You know, trauma?"

There was a silence in Rayanne's apartment for a little while, maybe five minutes. Their teas had gotten cold. Together they lifted their cups and tried to sip.

"Well," said Noor, "I hope this was some kind of therapy for you. All it did for me was make me feel creepy. I've got to go. Sandy will be getting worried."

"Just give me one more minute, Noor. I'm still not getting my point across."

"I can't believe this," Noor had uncrossed her legs. Now she crossed them again.

"See, it's not important whether I did kill the kittens or I didn't kill them."

"Well that makes a lot of sense. Why did you bring it up then?"

"The point is that I felt sorry for them!" Rayanne almost yelled at Noor. "I felt sorry for them. I hated what I did. Or thought I did. It bothered me then and it bothers me now."

Noor said nothing. She only looked at Rayanne with all the pity she could muster, and Noor was not a pitying sort of person. "I'm sorry," she said at last.

"No," said Rayanne, with a sigh. She dropped her chin and focused on the floor. "I'm still not being clear. What I'm trying to say is that when Elizabeth killed that chicken I looked at her face. No regret. No sorrow. There was not an ounce of pity in her whole body!"

Noor stood up. "O.K. I'm out of here. Tell me one of us doesn't need help."

Rayanne did not raise her head. Señor Cee wound himself around her legs.

The door closed. Rayanne heard the sound but all she could see through her tears was the boards of the bare wood floor, blurred and spreading, like thinner spilt on a fresh oil painting.

CHAPTER 31

▼

TENSION

For a few days things were strained between Noor and Rayanne. Maybe Noor was ashamed of herself for saying Rayanne needed counseling. Finally she brought Sandy over and introduced her, as perhaps a way of explaining herself or making a peace offering, Rayanne didn't know which.

They all went out to lunch. It was the Fish Market again, and the waiter's T-shirt still said "We serve crabs and a few nice people, too," but Rayanne no longer felt the promotion was funny or even quaint, and she resented it when Noor and Sandy wasted time talking about it. She resented even more having to pick up the check herself, especially since Noor had eaten enough for two. What was Noor's next surprise going to be, that she was pregnant?

But Rayanne knew down deep in her heart that picking up the tab was her way of telling Noor she forgave her. Somehow, awkward as the lunch had been, after a couple of soft shelled crab sandwiches and a couple of schooners of beer she felt she and Noor were buddies again.

Yes, they were buddies and it was official that they were buddies next day when Noor brought over the contact sheets for Rayanne to look at. Noor had also printed up exquisite 4x6's of her favorite images of Elizabeth and they lingered longest over these, discussing light and shadow and Elizabeth's expression. Jointly, at last, they agreed to telephone Rosemary, the hostess of the christening ceremony, who had commissioned Elizabeth's portrait.

A day later they had FedEx-ed the prints to her overnight, then Rosemary and Rayanne spent the better parts of three or four phone calls discussing the relative merits of the best of the prints. Finally, Rosemary delivered the heartbreaking news to Rayanne, "You know, I really hate it when paintings are done from a photograph. The problem is they always look like they're done from a photograph."

She went on to say that paintings from photos always look too contrasty. Actually she didn't say the word "contrasty." Instead she used lots of laymen's words that, in the end, meant "contrasty." Same with two-dimensional. Rosemary didn't like paintings that looked flat. She didn't use those words either, "two-dimensional" or "flat," but those were the words that her words meant.

There was one pose, though, that she liked, and a setting that she liked. Of course that was good news for Noor, because she was off the hook. But it was bad news for Rayanne. The setting was at Elizabeth's homeplace and the subject was, unavoidably, Elizabeth herself, the woman who had no qualms about wringing a chicken's neck. Maybe enjoyed it was putting it too strongly, but definitely no qualms. Definitely that.

CHAPTER 32

▼

ROAD

Rayanne felt a resolution forming inside her head. Her teeth clenched. She hated making resolutions. Resolutions were for overweight married women who needed to get a life. She was none of those.

But here she was once again depending on someone else for transportation. She needed to learn to drive.

Added to that was her feelings of guilt. Today it was Maddie who was driving her to Elizabeth's. She had offered Maddie a free lesson in exchange for the ride back out into Virginia farm country. Maddie was chattering away and Rayanne was stewing in a bath of guilt.

Mornings were always bad for her. Worse yet this particular morning she had started with a dream—a dream so vivid she woke early. It was still on her mind.

She had been at the window of her class room-studio, holding back, afraid of the broken pieces sticking out of the aged frame. From three stories up, looking sideways through the window frame, she could see below her the sprawled naked woman, face down, neck crooked, one arm underneath her body, puddles of blood snarling the concrete around her. Fragments of glass that the woman had pushed ahead of her and around her like a brittle wake lay sparkling and shiny in the sun. The beautiful rounded figure was now angular and flat. It would never have occurred to her to paint Elba that way. But it did occur to her then, in the dream.

Horrid image. God. Suddenly fragile, she was the smallest of the five women hurrying down the steps, the cool inside her dress billowing up from the pavement outdoors. At least the others were dressed for the street. Only her sneakers between her and the concrete, that and the thin fabric of the shift she wore. If they needed her dress for a bandage she'd have nothing to cover her. Nothing.

She was the last person down the steps. The four students stopped beside Elba's still form. Rayanne faintly heard or thought she heard Jasmine, the Corcoran student, say "I know CPR. I can do it." As she dropped beside the still form another voice said "I'm calling 911." Rayanne touched Elba's shoulders with fingers suddenly wet, tears falling dense and spattering off her nose.

She got someone to help her, and together, with one holding Elba's head and neck so they could turn her, and later with Jasmine administering CPR between her blowing sequences Ray's whole world was taken up with the flattened blood streaked face with its wild eyes and blue-grey forehead and the wetness of her own tears and hot cheeks and she knew Elba was already dead.

The dream continued, like a bad movie.

Detective Lieutenant Coelho ordered the sidewalk and the studio yellow taped. Their clothing was handed out to Rayanne's students, enough for them to make it home without risk of chill or exposure. None of their other personal gear was allowed out of the studio. The yellow tape remained.

"LSD. It was LSD. Where do they get LSD these days?" he asked.

Like a double dream, a dream-inside-a-dream, she was floating above him, thinking:

"No, LSD doesn't have that kind of effect, but anti-depressants do, anti-depressants used improperly. Could it be anti-depressants? Where would somebody like Elba get anti-depressants on zero income?"

Rayanne's lashes were sticky wet. Her cheeks, still hot, were crusted over from tears wiped every which way. She lowered herself off the stool. Barefooted she wandered around the studio, the warm, soft dust of the smooth old floorboards reassuring to the bottoms of her feet, sending that good feeling up her legs, like chills, only warm.

She looked at the model platform, at first sadly, then with compassion for this poor young woman and her brief life. Boyfriends, happiness, unhappiness. It was all over. She looked at the pillow against which Elba had lain. Its softness, where the folds still held from the press of the girl's body, reached out for her to touch it, but she had no need. Her eyes could feel the soft pillow, the stiff peaks of its rumpled creases, and the satin splotches of its damask relief.

She had no need, either, to touch the easels around the room, or the thin tracings of pencil upon them, shadows of the departed girl. The sense of graphite, at once oily and gritty, was in her fingers, instantly ignited by her eye's recollection. She knew that you can see the artist in every drawing from his hand. She had only to look at what they had left behind on their easels to see inside of her the grief, the fright and the pain of four women around the damaged body of Elba. They couldn't have caused her death. Every torn, wretched face was genuine, she knew.

She worked through the dream—as if she were being forced to relive every wretched moment.

These four students of hers were honest women. Women who'd studied with her long years, and many sessions. Honest women, doing honest work on their canvasses. Women who trusted her, who had gone with her down many paths in drawing and painting, who now followed her into her blue period. Whose brushes and pencils lay on the trays below their canvasses, the tips of the instruments facing left if they were right handed, otherwise right. Women whose tubes of oils were ready with the blues for this coming phase into which they were all to plunge together—Phthalocyanine blue, cobalt blue, manganese blue, cerulean blue and indanthrone blue …

She went out into the hall and put coins in the wall payphone. "That detective," she told Maddie, forcing out the words through a thickening throat, "he wants each of you to come and get your canvas. I don't know why."

In her dream they sat then, the two of them, Maddie's curl straying over her forehead as she shook her head slowly from side to side and, when their eyes met, each saw the other's pain and fresh tears came.

"She was such a sweet girl," said Rayanne in a faint and sad little voice. Maddie nodded. She worked her jaw sideways to break the flow of tears. "That man, Coelho, said you knew her from before."

"Yeah," said Maddie. She pulled a rumpled handkerchief again from a front jeans pocket. "We worked together."

"No kidding?"

"Yeah, before I was riffed." Maddie raised her chin, so she could look at Rayanne without crying.

"Did you hate her?"

Maddie continued to meet Rayanne's eyes for what seemed like a long time. Ray-anne thought she should look away, but it was Maddie who looked away. First she looked away, then she looked down at her hands fidgeting in her lap, twisting a damp wadded handkerchief.

"She was a whistle blowin' big fat snitch. We all lost our jobs. Wasn't another department would hire a one of us."

Rayanne tried to look brave. "You didn't really mean her to die, did you?"

A frightened Maddie's eyes, staring. "No. No. Really. Not die! Not on that stuff. That's the stuff keeps me going. Nobody knows what it's like staying home. Kids. Meals. Cleaning. Shit." They sat together in silence. Rayanne looking at the floor, the warm dusty floor. In her mind she saw a large flattened body, all crooked.

"She was a big girl. I thought it would take a whole lot more than with me. I just gave her a whole lot more. I didn't know. How could I know? Jesus!"

Rayanne felt herself drawing up her feet under her, pulling back into herself. Away from this woman. This murderess, this painter with her easel and its sketching pencils pointing every which way.

"So, like she'd act stupid. She'd do something weird. It would be, like, revenge. You know?"

In her dream she had solved Elba's death but she was not happy.

Coelho asked her about it. It was the blues, she told him, a case of the blues they'd all been taking tubes of paint from. Madeline had to have been distracted, must have been thinking of something else. The only blue she had pulled was the ultramarine. Five tubes, all the same … and not much like a blue at all. O.K. with other colors, but not with other blues. Really an ugly shade of blue.

Maybe it was some kind of closure, but it did not make her happy. In her heart she knew she did not have the right answer. She awoke crying.

*   *   *   *

By the time Rayanne and Maddie were set up at Elizabeth's, easels side by side, Rayanne had put Elba out of her mind, but not very far. Somehow these days the thought of Elba was always with her.

Rosemary had chosen a pose for Elizabeth where she was backlighted by the dining area's windows. They were large windows divided by a lattice work of framing into small squares. Under these conditions Elizabeth's face would be in a faint shadow.

CHAPTER 33

▼

MY ELBA?

"Dear, you seem distracted."

Rayanne felt herself shifting her attention away from Elizabeth's whole face and onto Elizabeth's eyes—in the same face. It was a particularly strange feeling.

Maddie had already done all she could with her canvas and gone outside leaving an abstract-looking stiffly posed elderly woman staring out of her canvas into the room. Now they could hear the higher notes of Maddie's chatter reaching them from the garden where she was apparently talking to Ferlin about weeding.

"Who me?" asked Rayanne, mentally kicking herself because there was no one else in the room for Elizabeth to be talking about. She went on without giving Elizabeth time for the reply she wasn't going to make anyway.

"I ... well, yes, I guess I was daydreaming. I do that when I paint. I really do. Sometimes. Sometimes I just drift off ... oh, it doesn't affect my work. I mean, painting is automatic ... no, what I really mean, it's second nature to me. It's what I do best ... you know." She finished lamely and hated herself for sounding apologetic. This woman wasn't even paying her. Why try to justify herself to Elizabeth?

"Oh, I'm sure your work is just beautiful," Elizabeth said. "Don't dare show it to me till it's finished, though. I want to be surprised."

She's fishing, Rayanne thought. What does she want?

"But I am curious," Elizabeth continued. "I think you are troubled. What is troubling you?"

"Me? Oh, no. I'm not troubled. I was just thinking about somebody."

"Who, dear?"

Now this old woman's being patronizing, Rayanne thought, but her mind wasn't working fast enough to come up with an evasion, so she panicked and told the truth. "I was thinking about someone, a model at the Art League, someone I used to paint."

"Someone I know?"

"Well, probably not," Rayanne abstractedly dipped her brush and drew it out, loading it lightly. "She didn't live anywhere around here. Her name was Elba."

"Elba Houston?"

"Why, yes! How did you know?"

"I know her parents. They live over in Front Royal."

"I had no idea," said Rayanne. She could think of nothing else to say. She began to re-load her brush. Then questions began to swirl in her head. She didn't want to ask any of them.

Elizabeth, however, could not be stopped. "You said 'was.' You said her name 'was' Elba. Why did you say 'was'? Did she change her name … like your other friend—Noor?"

Was there anything this woman didn't know?

Rayanne felt a creature inside her shouting, Ask Miz Know-It-All to answer herself, but instead she said, quietly, "She died."

For a long minute she thought she had spoken too softly. Maybe the woman hadn't heard. At last Elizabeth spoke.

"I'm sorry to hear that. What did she die of?" Then to herself, as if in afterthought, "She was so young."

"She fell out a window … at the Art League." Rayanne couldn't bring herself this time to tell the truth. She didn't want to share anything with Elizabeth about the police department's so-called suicide.

"That's such a shame," said Elizabeth. "Such a sad life, yet she was doing so well."

"What do you mean, 'doing so well'?" Rayanne was surprised to hear herself asking. Elizabeth's remark had a kind of clinical sound, as if she were somehow involved in Elba's actual life.

Elizabeth's eyes widened. Rayanne pulled the brush away from the canvas as her model's expression changed under her hand.

"Why, my dear, she used to come to me!"

CHAPTER 34

▼

WHY ELBA?

"It was all I could do to finish what I had blocked in for that session," Rayanne said to Noor.

It was the next day. The two of them were walking past the historic home of Robert E. Lee that the city of Alexandria had recently sold into private hands in a backroom deal. Neither General Lee nor Northern Virginia politics was on their minds as they focused on the problem of Rayanne and her latest portrait job.

Rayanne had indeed finished the rough shapes and colors of Elizabeth's face with a general once-over of the windowed background behind her sitter's seated figure. It was lucky for Rayanne that Elizabeth had begun to tire noticeably. The two hour sitting they had agreed upon had taken its toll and Elizabeth really seemed to want to lie down.

Rayanne didn't understand about this business of Elba being a friend of Elizabeth's way out in Virginia farm country. And Ferlin, he had looked strange and acted strange when she and Maddie were there working on Elizabeth's portrait.

"Looked strange? How?," asked Noor.

"I don't know," said Rayanne. "Just strange. He had seemed so young and strong last time. This time he seemed weakly and thin. Maybe older, too."

"Did he look tired?"

"No. Like I said, he was just acting strange."

"Well? You'd act strange too if you were his age stuck with somebody like her."

"No, that's what I'm trying to tell you. He seemed really happy. Kind of delirious, in a way. Like he was wanting to dance out in the yard. You know, kind of light-headed."

CHAPTER 35

▼

CARLENE TOO?

There was no escaping her obligation. Rayanne had to go back for the second sitting with Elizabeth. That's was what she was paid to do. She was not looking forward to the trip. In a way she was glad that Maddie was not free today, what with children and errands keeping her house-bound. Rayanne felt she was lucky to have found Philip free and able to drive her out there.

Philip was retired from government work, which meant he was probably close to 60 years old, but still healthy and fit. Somehow she felt a little safer having him driving her. The first session with Elizabeth had been emotionally challenging and, while she couldn't exactly say she had been afraid or even anxious during that sitting, she felt distinctly relieved to have Philip with her for this next sitting.

Rayanne and Maddie had gotten lost a couple of times on the last visit, and maybe for that reason she had paid more careful attention or maybe it was just the warmth of Phil's presence, but she felt more confident now and directed him flawlessly to Elizabeth's house with an air of new-found authority.

Ferlin seemed to be hard at work in the front garden when they drove up. When she introduced the two men she noticed that Ferlin seemed to have aged even more since her last visit. He looked thinner, if that were possible, and she could have sworn there were noticeable white hairs when he took off his hat where it had been all dark brown before. On the other hand he seemed happy and animated, almost manic, when he greeted them.

She left the two men talking and went in to start her session with Elizabeth. There was a freshly made cup of tea on the table and the chair and window decorations were just as she had left them. Elizabeth easily moved into the now-familiar pose.

Rayanne set up her easel and got to work with a strong feeling of emptiness inside her. She realized she was missing the camaraderie of Maddie's presence and found herself filling the empty space where Maddie's easel had been with a ghostly image of the cheerful young dark haired woman in her smock busily working away with brush and oils.

There was no music playing. Rayanne could have used some music in the background. Some Bach would have been nice. Or some Mozart. It was so damned quiet in this kitchen-dining-living room that she would have even settled for some Flatt and Scruggs—well, maybe not too loud.

At last Elizabeth spoke into the silence.

"Dear?" That word again. Rayanne look directly into Elizabeth's eyes, eyebrows lifted.

"You told me during your last visit that Elba's death was one of three."

Rayanne nodded. Elizabeth was looking directly at her now, her face tilted out of the pose. She would have to get Elizabeth back into the pose.

"Who were the other two?"

"Oh, they weren't anybody you would have known. They were models down at the Art League."

Elizabeth continued to look at Rayanne, her face turned even farther out of the pose. The silent command hung in the air.

"Well, one was a girl, named Carlene Kohlmeyer. The other was a boy, a young man named David-Mark Phlinders."

"I'm sorry to hear about their passing over. No, I never knew any David-Mark."

Elizabeth closed her eyes, then deliberately and carefully turned her head back into precisely the right position for the pose. She opened her eyes and assumed exactly the same serene look as before.

"I did know Carlene, though," she said evenly. "She came here with Elba."

CHAPTER 36

▼

REMINISCED

Phil was not given to talkativeness and the drive back to Alexandria was endured pretty much in silence. He had not even turned the radio on, so Rayanne was free to think over this latest episode in the long dark tunnel of horrors that began with Carlene's beautiful neck elongated and obscene, hanging from the studio bathroom ceiling.

Rayanne had been barely able to finish this latest session with Elizabeth. The brush in her hand felt as if it weighed a hundred pounds. It was warm, no, it was hot in the room. So hot she could hardly breathe. And there was Elizabeth wearing long sleeves. What was it with Elizabeth and Ferlin and those long sleeves in this weather?

Her brush added the necessary details to Elizabeth's face as if running on autopilot. This had not been her best work.

She was surprised when Elizabeth told her why Elba and Carlene had visited her. People, Elizabeth had said, especially young women, need a wise person to counsel them as they start life on their own. At my age, she said, I am a crone, someone who has lived a long time—then she went on with something about herbs, advice, understanding. Herbs, herbs, herbs.

Now in the car, Rayanne rested her head on the seat back and wondered about Elba and Carlene. She had never thought of the two of them as connected in any way. Now she needed to think. She tried to remember all she could about Carlene. It wasn't much. A classic modern fashion model's body.

Carlene had also been toned, she remembered. Carlene could raise some muscles when she flexed. But mostly Carlene had been easy going, composed and distant most of the time. Personality of a turnip, Rayanne had thought in those days and nothing came out of her soul-searching to change her mind.

Elba, on the other hand, had been a vibrating, vocal, almost boisterous personality. Rayanne had always felt electrified in her presence, had always looked forward to having her pose. Could remember the time she'd gone to Elba's group house …

CHAPTER 37

▼

GROUP HOUSE

It had been a hot day when Rayanne went to visit Elba at her group house. A very hot, very muggy Northern Virginia summer day. Looking back on it now, Rayanne couldn't remember why she had gone on that particular day. Maybe part of it had been to see if the house had changed since she had lived there. Maybe it had been as much to see the house as to see Elba. Otherwise Elba could have come to her, come to the Art Center, if it had been on Center business, or to Rayanne's studio apartment if it had been something personal.

Personal? No, it would have been too early in their acquaintanceship for that. Well, she would try later to remember why she had gone. For now it was enough just to remember what the house had been like, and what Elba had been like on that day.

The house had stood on a corner of South St. Asaph, maybe five or six blocks from where Rayanne lived and taught art classes. It was a short, brisk walk on a bright spring day or in early fall when the leaves were turning and the cobble-stones of Prince Street were copper in the late afternoon sun and rolled like a massage comfortably underfoot. Brisk then and cheery, but on a hot, humid summer day it was a slow sweaty walk at any speed up Prince Street from the water front and down St. Asaph to this southeast corner.

The building may once have been a plantation home or at least a plantation owner's vision of what a gracious in-town home should be. There were wide porches on all sides of the first two floors. The porches were open on three of the sides and closed on the back of the house. The placement and size of the kitchen conveyed a general air of a long severed connection to what must have been slaves' quarters, on space now occupied by other people's houses. Structurally the house may have been tied to plantation days, but socially it was closer to a beach scene.

Through the front gate, inside the concrete fence on either side there were blankets spread here and there on the grass and occupied, or in some cases recently occupied, by young women engaged in the peripheral activities of sunbathing.

There were girls lying on their stomachs, backs glistening wet with either perspiration or lotion or both, some with bikini straps tied, some untied. One or two looked up at her, most were oblivious. One young woman lay on her back, a towel draped over her eyes. She raised one corner of her towel to check out Rayanne walking by.

There were at least two radios playing on different blankets. They were the ghetto blaster type of portable radios, probably a couple of feet long each, black, bulky and intimidating. They were set to different radio stations but were set to mercifully low volumes. Perhaps the discordance was only audible to someone like Rayanne, briefly caught between them.

Some of the blankets displayed the wreckage of interrupted sun baths. Unoccupied except for bottles of lotion, scraps of letters recently read or written, their pages limp in the humid air, soggy paperback novels forgotten on the grass, and sewn into one blanket with what looked to be a seven foot-long cartoon character against a white background, some hairbrushes and a comb with long, widely spaced teeth. A tapered bottle of dark pink nail polish teetered on the blanket's edge, where it might have been used for toenails, about to fall into the grass.

Rayanne felt she must have known some of the young women, there were at least five or six of them on the occupied blankets, but only a couple had looked at her, and she hadn't caught any faces she recognized. The female body, she had decided, face down and flat against the ground, butt spread saggily from hip to hip, did not offer much to engage a person's artistic interests.

In any case she had not expected to see Elba out here, so she went inside.

The front door was ajar. Inside the air was as muggy as outside, only darker. The main hall served as a holding room for the central stair and for almost nothing else except the remnants of a once elaborate chandelier, and a large television set to one side with several folding chairs, no two alike, and what appeared to be sofa cushions lying about on the bare floor.

There was a ball game on the screen, she couldn't now remember whether it was football or soccer, but it was something involving striped grass and a lot of noise. There was a guy sitting in one of the chairs, watching. He had a sweating beer can in his hand, with a couple of empties sitting in puddles on the floor beside him, and he was smoking. He did not look up as she passed through the collection of chairs.

She went into the kitchen through the door that she remembered behind the stairs. Elba had promised to meet her there. Rayanne was exactly on time, as she now recalled. Probably it would have been eleven o'clock, that would have been a good time to get together with a twenty-somethings woman in a group house for an early morning talk.

Being on time meant she'd have to wait a quarter of an hour or so for Elba to show. She sat down at the table, on the long side where she could see the door into the hall that she had just come out of, into the dining room and out into the back yard, all without turning around.

It was the same table that had been there when she lived in the house. She thrilled for a moment to this one feeling of familiarity, after all of the new faces outside, and the uncomfortable sense of accelerating deterioration all around her.

As she sat and waited a young woman walked through from the hallway, in a t-shirt and jeans, barefoot, her eyes puffy from sleep, hair unbrushed, trailing a bath towel behind her, part of it dragging along the floor. The girl didn't look her way but shuffled out the screen door, letting it slam behind her.

Rayanne heard a faint thumping noise above her head and realized now that just such a sound had preceded the first girl's entrance. Another girl came through, also heading out the back. She looked vaguely in Rayanne's direction. "You seen my cigarettes?"

Rayanne's eyes widened in surprise.

"Marlboros." The girl said. "Guess not."

And "Shit."

The girl walked out. The screen banged again.

"Can't stand that noise!" a man's voice called from the dining room.

After a while Rayanne got up and went over to the dining room door. There was no dining table or any other real furniture, but in the middle of the room there were sawhorses with a couple of what appeared to be one-by-twelves lying on them. A young man with a Van Dyke beard and no shirt was bending over the makeshift work table drawing out a poster or some other kind of a sign, using Magic Markers.

He was making circles along the edges of lettering he had already lined up, in a sort of bubble effect. She could see now that the letters and the bubbles were drawn to look as if they were escaping from a beer bottle lying on its side, with a puddle of something around it. He raised his head. He had pale blue eyes.

"I don't know. What do you think?" He straightened up so he could turn to face her. "Looks like shit, don't it?"

He had used neon colors, and had used highlighting and shadows in contrasted tones to give his bubbles a three dimensional effect. It was, well, nauseating.

"Nice," she lied. "A party?"

"Yeah, Elba's," he said, bending down again to his work. "Got a job. Modeling."

God, Rayanne thought. She thinks this is a job? Elba must have landed, if "landed" was the right word, a total of three three-hour posing sessions for Rayanne's class over a three week period. One three-hour session on each of three succeeding weeks. At ten dollars an hour, that came to ninety dollars over three weeks, period.

She was curious. "Who's buying the beer?"

"Who do you think?" he asked, without looking up. "Elba's the one's got the job. So guess which one of us's got the money."

Shit, Rayanne thought. It'd cost Elba all her modeling just buying beer for this house. How do these people live? She had forgotten already what it was like.

He straightened up again and looked at her more critically. He reached to one side and picked up a pair of glasses. One of the stems was broken off. He held them to his face with his free hand. "You wanna hang out or something till I'm finished here?"

She figured he was about ten years younger than she was, maybe just out of high school. She smiled then laughed—warmly, she hoped.

"That'd be fun," she said, "but it'd have to be another time. I'm here to see Elba today."

He looked puzzled.

"Elba," she said again.

He still looked puzzled. One hand went to his Van Dyke. It was the one with the neon red Magic Marker in it. She thought he was going to streak his face, but he missed. He pulled rhythmically at the point of his beard. She watched fascinated at the Magic Marker rode up and down, up and down, the wet end just missing his lips and nose.

"It's about her new job," she said, "I'm teaching the art class."

"No stuff?" he said. "I thought you were kind of new lookin'."

He leaned his head back.

"Hey, Elba!" he yelled out. "Get your fat ass down here!"

*   *   *   *

Rayanne thought about that day. She thought about Elizabeth and Ferlin in their long sleeves. She thought about what Elizabeth had said to her when she killed that chicken and Elizabeth had seen the stricken look on her face.

"It's the blood, isn't it, dear? Blood should not upset you. Blood is the life force. When you have it you are alive in this world. When you do not have it you return to the earth from which you came."

Her hand had indicated the other chickens nervously pecking apart the head of their sister hen. The eyes were already gone.

"Sometimes," Elizabeth had added, "we have too much blood in us. We get high strung. Everyone needs to relax. Blood is not always in balance."

Rayanne straightened up in the car seat. Like a blank canvas you look at and suddenly you see an idea, fully formed. She knew what she had to do.

CHAPTER 38

▼

UP CLOSE

Rayanne looked long and critically in the mirror at the face looking back at her. The squarish jaw, she decided, was okay. She would have rather had an oval face. Oval was what she taught. But squarish was okay. She peered closely at the freckles sprinkled lightly over the bridge of her nose and on either side just under her eyes.

Yes, a careful stroke or two of foundation artistically applied, foundation that matched the color of her neck where it hadn't tanned, that very light use of foundation would conceal those silly freckles. Yep, they'd hide 'em all right, whenever she would have to go out where "out," in this case, mean the world outside the world of art.

Rayanne's view of life, of people, and of purpose, she had to admit to herself in this case—there was no one else around—was driven by emotion and by instinct. No way to get around it. That was what she was. A creature of emotion. No better than a happy puppy, tail wagging when things worked right. And mean as a dog when you grabbed his bone, if things went wrong.

A creature of instinct. The choices she made in her life, and there were a lot of bad ones, were choices she made because … well she didn't know why.

"Instinct," she said out loud. "Instinct."

It was her instinct that made her draw what she drew, paint what she painted, and know what was good when she made it good. And instinct, she decided, was what she had to work with. Instinct was what was going to help her get these deaths out of her life. She would figure out this mess for herself, and she would figure it out by intuition, not in that stupid step by step way that Coelho used and definitely not by sitting down and working through things analytically, whatever that meant.

This was a big moment she decided later, the big moment. What some people call a turning point. It was a turning point in her life.

What she had seen in the mirror and what she felt inside, these were the only forces she had to work with, but these were the forces that would help her find the answer—her way.

CHAPTER 39

▼

WICCA

On a Sunday morning Noor was not fond of being rousted out of bed. True, she could be more jovial when her eyes first opened than Rayanne could be after spending hours getting coffeed up through breakfast and lunch together, but still she had not been wildly enthusiastic when Rayanne hit her door like a drug bust at ten AM and kidnapped her for nothing more exciting than a pre-noon visit to the National Gallery of Art.

The Mellon Gallery, as long-time Washingtonians call it, sits on the north side of the Mall, about a third of the way from the Capitol to the White House. There had been a brief power struggle between Noor and Rayanne which Noor won, meaning they drove over from Alexandria, a fifteen minute trip, then spent half an hour looking for a parking space.

If Rayanne had won they would have traveled by Metro, emerging from underground a couple of hundred yards from the Museum, free of parking worries, but it would have taken twice as long and they would have had to share their Metro car with countless sticky-fingered kids and near-hysterical parents.

Noor could have stayed home. She and Sandy had no particular plans but what embryonic expectations they may have had for the day certainly did not include a frantic trip to an art museum. Sandy listened to Rayanne's begging and pleading till she could hardly stand it. She watched in growing disbelief as Noor gradually began to cave in, then suggested, in an overloud voice more appropriate to a Marine Corps parade ground than to their small apartment, that Rayanne and Noor both do something physically impossible to themselves, grabbed up the Sunday edition of *The Washington Post* from the coffee table and slammed the bedroom door on them.

Rayanne's adrenaline had hit dry bottom about the time they crossed Memorial Bridge and she was in serious need of caffeine by the time they got inside the building. On the second floor was a charming fern-garnished gathering spot with little metal tables and garden chairs where a college-age waiter would bring you coffee. That was where they landed, that was what they ordered and that was when Noor demanded the real reason why she had been shanghaied. Rayanne was no better prepared to explain now than she had been earlier at Sandy's and Noor's apartment.

"Does this really have something to do with those suicides?"

"Murders."

"Whatever."

"Noor, the answers are here. They're here."

"Rayanne, I truly believe you really are as crazy as Sandy says you are."

"We may need her."

"What? You want somebody's nose busted?"

"It's not that. I think we've got to save Ferlin's life."

"Who?"

"Ferlin. You know, the guy that's married to Elizabeth. You know, the portrait. The pose from the photograph you made. The one I'm painting."

"That's it. You are crazy."

"No, no, no. I believe he's being killed and doesn't know it."

"You want me to send in my lover, a former Marine, to save the life of somebody that no one knows is dying?"

"Be serious, Noor. Please."

"You're the one that's not being serious, Rayanne. Am I the only friend you've got? I'm beginning to think so. I'm also beginning to think you're about to lose the last friend you've got."

"Just give me one hour, Noor. That's all I ask. Just one hour. If you don't want to help me, after I've showed you the proof, then just write me off, and write off this whole business."

"You're not going to believe this, Rayanne, but I wrote off this thing about the suicides, murders, from the very beginning. It's not likely you're going to change my mind about that."

"Will you just stay with me for one hour, though, like I asked?"

"Yes, but only for you, not for this silly idea of yours, Rayanne. I'm sorry."

"O. K. That's all I ask. Just hang on for one hour."
"Right."
Why did Noor have to spoil it by saying "Right?"

CHAPTER 40

▼

SECRETS

An anxious Rayanne led the way down the vaulted hallway, away from the coffee lounge. Noor dragged along, about half a step behind.

Rayanne picked an archway, stepped quickly past a guy in uniform, then pulled back, leaving a very puzzled man on guard.

"Sorry. Not here."

The next archway was the right one. She stopped in front of the guard on duty and waved Noor inside, like a kindergarten teacher on a field trip. The painting she pointed to was called "The Medical Patient."

"See?" said Rayanne. "You gotta admit, it's all there."

"This is not an explanation of something, Rayanne. This is not even a clue. It's a painting. Just a bunch of guys looking at somebody's body."

"Look at it, Noor. Look at it."

The guard had left the doorway and was coming over.

Rayanne lowered her voice, and in a growling stage whisper urged "Look at the arms, Noor. Look at his arms."

Noor looked. The guard looked. Then they both looked at Rayanne.

"Don't you see?" asked Rayanne.

Noor shook her head. The guard continued to look at Rayanne.

Rayanne grabbed Noor's arm and pulled her away from the painting and the puzzled-looking guard. "It's the arms, don't you see the puncture wounds?"

"Yes ... yes," said Noor. Then, "*Yes!*"
"And the bucket?"

CHAPTER 41

NEXT IMAGE

"Rayanne," said Noor. "I think I see a little, but it doesn't explain much."

They were hurrying down the long, vaulted hallway now, going in the opposite direction, headed for the stairs. Even Noor was beginning to show some excitement. She was like a puppy who was caught up in the energy of the chase but not yet clear just what animal they were chasing.

Two floors below, Rayanne darted into another exhibition room, hurrying too fast for the comfort level of the guard on duty. He moved quickly into step behind them, as if expecting Rayanne to pull an ink pot out of her dress pocket at any moment and throw it up onto one of his precious charges. Noor tried to give him a reassuring smile as she passed but he continued to follow them into the room, only walking a little slower.

This painting was entitled "Oberon and Titania." Rayanne stretched out a finger and pointed triumphantly, "See? What did I tell you?"

Doing her best to be supportive, Noor could barely manage a tentative smile of the weakest sort of encouragement. How does one encourage a lunatic was probably the closest approximation to the look she gave Rayanne.

"Don't you see? Titania is queen of the fairies. All the other fairies look up to her. She's their leader. She is the center of their world. She is the one who knows everything. She is the wise woman."

Noor turned her gaze on Rayanne. Noor's eyes had never looked so brown, Rayanne thought. Why had she never noticed how deep a brown Noor's eyes were?

Noor said, "If I understand right you think everything should be clear now that I've seen two paintings. I think you think these two paintings are evidence of a crime. Rayanne, I don't know any more about crime than what I see on T. V. and read in the papers, but I don't think two paintings at the National Gallery of Art in Washington, D. C., are evidence about three crimes in Alexandria, or a criminal who lives somewhere out in Loudon County, Virginia."

Rayanne's eyes began to burn and her cheeks flushed hot. She knew that the next thing would be tears. She stiffened her back and looked up at Noor. "Will you go with me? Out to Elizabeth's house?"

Noor did not answer.

Rayanne asked again, not moving away from Noor's face, "Would you do it for me?"

No response.

"I think Ferlin is dying. Will you do it for him?"

Noor turned away from her. "I don't have a gun. Let's see. Sandy is a trained killer …"

"We'll take her with us."

CHAPTER 42

▼

SCENE

Ferlin was not in the garden or any place else that was visible from the front of the house. They left Sandy in the car.

It was now early afternoon and warm. Sandy rolled down the windows. She watched them climb the front steps and knock on the door. She picked up the Sunday sports section and started reading.

Listening for footsteps, Rayanne felt small and lonely, even with Noor standing next to her.

Rayanne and Noor had debated calling Coelho on the way over to pick up Sandy, then the three of them debated it again on the way out of town. They finally agreed that Rayanne should not file a complaint about something she had not herself actually witnessed.

Sandy pointed out that conjecture was not evidence and, really, they didn't have anything. She also pointed out that Elizabeth and Ferlin, as described by Noor and Rayanne, did not seem dangerous and certainly the elderly woman they kept talking about did not sound like any sort of a physical threat to two healthy, robust, younger women.

Rayanne, who had never thought of herself as robust, believed with all her heart that Noor could take care of herself, but she was not certain who could take care of Rayanne. She was a little bit comforted in her mind as she pictured Ferlin, in his broad straw hat, tight blue jeans, clodhoppers and checkered long-sleeved shirt and had to agree with Sandy that he did not seem threatening. Nor even intimidating.

On the other hand, Rayanne's mental image of Elizabeth produced a formidable, if not exactly threatening, presence. Plus, there was the physical strength it took to wring the chicken's neck. This last image she desperately wanted to suppress. She was glad to find they were already at the farm and ready to confront her nemesis.

It unnerved Rayanne to find Ferlin absent, but they had deliberately not called ahead so there was no reason to expect Elizabeth to station him out front, if that was her habit with guests.

To Rayanne's discomfort Elizabeth herself answered the door.

"Well, hello, my dears," she said pulling the door wider. "Come right in. I wasn't expecting you the least little bit."

Somehow they found themselves seated in the dining-sitting room. Elizabeth was in the place of her pose, with the windows behind her. The room was over-warm as usual and, as usual, Elizabeth was wearing long sleeves.

"We were driving by …," began Noor.

"Actually, I asked Noor to drive me out here. I was worried …," Rayanne cut in.

"About me?"

"Oh, no. I mean about Elba and Carlene."

"You told me they were dead." Elizabeth's tone was icy.

CHAPTER 43

▼

CITY GIRLS

"They are dead," said Rayanne.

"Well, then?" Elizabeth arched her eyebrows, not theatrically but just enough.

"Oh, I just have this awful time trying to explain what I mean," said Rayanne. "It happens all the time."

Elizabeth folded her hands in her lap. An air of benign patience flowed out of her and suffused the room.

"Well, you see, Elba and Carlene … well, they were city girls, and …"

"Why would they need to come all the way out here?" Elizabeth prodded.

"Well …," started Rayanne.

"Yes!" interjected Noor, finishing the thought for Rayanne, and mirroring the impatience she seemed sure Elizabeth was beginning to feel.

Rayanne really wished other people wouldn't do her thinking for her, much less do her talking for her.

"I told you," said Elizabeth, with just a little more firmness than necessary. "I am friends with Elba's parents. They live here in Loudon County."

"Even so," Rayanne was feeling a little stubborn now herself, "she was an artist's model and lived down in the city. Somehow I can't see her … here."

"People come to me for help," said Elizabeth. Now her tone had a slightly strident edge. "Perhaps you don't understand the kind of counsel an older woman has to offer."

"About modeling? About boyfriends? About roommates? What?" Rayanne was surprised to hear herself asking.

"About life, my dear."

"Yes, but Elba was just a girl. There's such a … difference … between you."

"Elba had many problems. She had many concerns. I am particularly good at helping with problems, with stress."

Noor butted in again. "Are you a yoga person?"

"No."

"Are you, like, a Druid?"

Elizabeth laughed. It was almost a laugh-out-loud kind of laugh. Rayanne felt a chill, it was so unexpected.

"How foolish you are, Noor, dear. You must be thinking of Montana Louise's christening. Maybe it seemed Druidic to you, but the ceremony was not Druidic, believe me. It was Wicca."

"What's the difference?" asked the ever-practical Noor. It was her habit to ask for and to expect hard answers. That was her only way of dealing with things. Not for her were the hazy, half-realized ideas and notions of the Rayannes of this world.

"Oh, there are differences, but they are not important. Elba's needs and those of her friend Carlene had no connection to Wicca. Elba and Carlene were suffering from very difficult experiences, stresses and … depression. Problems that require the kinds of help that can only come from knowledge far older than Wicca and the Druids."

What kind of person would talk this way, Rayanne wondered. Were they in the presence of a madwoman? Or was Elizabeth just stringing them along?

CHAPTER 44

▼

CRONE

"They are dead," Rayanne repeated.

"Well, Dear, wouldn't it be best to let the dead rest?

"I can't do that."

"I see that you can't. You are very troubled about those two young women, aren't you?"

"Yes, I am. They were my friends."

"Let's sit and talk about them, then. After all, they were my friends, too."

"They were? Your friends?"

"You seem surprised," Elizabeth said, raising her eyebrows in what seemed to Rayanne a most intimidating manner.

"Well, it's just that I thought ..."

"That I was so much older? That we could not possibly have been friends?"

"Well, yes, I guess you could say that," Rayanne could feel herself getting more intimidated by the minute, yet somewhere she could just barely feel a grain of courage. She felt, with luck, it might be in her to nourish that tiny grain just a little bit.

"It's true," Elizabeth continued, "they did come to see me in my official capacity. Let me fix us some tea."

"An official capacity?" Rayanne could sense Noor rolling her eyes and realized she had begun to echo Elizabeth's words. I'll work on improving my conversational skills later, she thought. Right now I've got all I can do just to keep my courage up.

"I am a crone," Elizabeth said, a strange mixture of pride and apology in her voice. "I have lived a long time and people come to me for advice. Life is a puzzle that many people have trouble figuring out. Especially the very young." She walked away from them, over to the stove, moving slowly, but strangely erect. The cumulative effect was like a tree or some tall landscape planting, being carried upright by a very careful and sensitive gardener.

"I'm sorry," Rayanne was irritated by the sound of her own apologetic voice, "it's just that they are both dead and they both came to see you ... was it about the same time?"

"Oh, yes," Elizabeth answered quickly. "Let's see, I believe it was Elba who introduced Carlene to me. They came here together. A particularly nice young man drove them. Afterwards he came back a few times by himself. He had an unusual first name. There was a hyphen in it ..."

She hesitated, while her memory worked. Her expression carried new concern. She looked at Rayanne. "You know I believe you mentioned his name to me. I didn't recognize it at the time ..."

Rayanne heard herself and Elizabeth saying the name together, "David-Mark."

CHAPTER 45

▼

FERLIN

"Yes, David-Mark was his name," said Elizabeth. "How foolish of me to forget." She drew herself up as if regathering her strength.

"Yes," said Rayanne quietly. "He used to model for my class."

"Now he's dead?" asked Elizabeth.

Now. Yes, now, Rayanne found herself thinking. At last Elizabeth has faced the truth. What will Noor think of that? Somehow she did not feel triumphant. Neither did she want to glance at Noor to see what her reaction had been. The two of them by now had cups of tea in their hands, and all three were waiting expectantly. It dawned on Rayanne that she had been hoping someone else would answer Elizabeth's question.

"Yeah," Noor spoke into the vacuum. "He's dead, too."

The lines of Elizabeth's face tightened, as if she were setting her teeth against some imminent challenge. Or maybe it was in response to some unpleasant suspicion. In any case her face set into some impregnable determination.

"I'm sorry to hear that," Elizabeth said at last. "He had been through some difficult times and his disposition had begun to seem so cheerful."

"Can't see that," said Noor. "The kid committed suicide."

Rayanne would not have put it so baldly, but she found herself nodding too readily in agreement, and her nose started to redden, a sure sign of tears to follow shortly.

"That is very sad," said Elizabeth. "I can hardly believe it."

For a moment Elizabeth's face seemed to open to them, as if the rigid determination of a few moments earlier had softened, and she seemed to be focusing inward. She spoke as if trying to reassure herself, "They were so young. So full of promise. They went through some bad times, but so does everyone else. They only needed to feel better about themselves, to see the world around them in a brighter way. They only needed to feel real happiness for a short while ..."

Her voice trailed off. Her features gathered up the sense of determination around her. Resolution shone out of her eyes. She spoke firmly.

"It's too bad. Three nice young people. All they needed was to see what it was like, even for just a moment, to feel good about themselves."

Neither Rayanne nor Noor spoke. They were spellbound, each wondering in her own way about Elizabeth. How could she know so much? How could she be both uninvolved in these young peoples' lives and involved? Passive agent? Active agent?

"They did come to see the world as a happy place. I know they did. I know it." She raised her chin, almost proudly.

Rayanne and Noor did not speak.

"I don't know what happened after that," Elizabeth added then, and it seemed her chest relaxed. For a moment there was almost a sense of defeat, as if Rayanne and Noor had watched a battle take place and were seeing the aftereffects.

She seemed to return to the present. She looked at Rayanne and Noor. "I don't know what happened to either of them."

"To any one of the three," she corrected herself, as if to reassure someone. Them? Herself? That she was in charge.

"Why would they commit suicide if they were happy?" Rayanne was surprised at herself. Where had her sudden spark of courage come from? Was it from Elizabeth's momentary loss of composure? Had she, Rayanne, out of nowhere, developed an instinct for the jugular? The image shook her, yet she held onto it. Somehow it was beginning to seem relevant.

"My dear," said Elizabeth, the old spirit came back, intensified, "I'm sure I don't know."

But Rayanne was not intimidated this time. She surprised herself.

"Where's Ferlin?" she found herself blurting. Noor turned and stared at Rayanne as if Rayanne had suddenly arrived from another planet.

"Ferlin, dear?" Elizabeth looked surprised also, but unlike Noor she did not lose her composure.

"He would be about his chores, dear," Elizabeth added, but it was lamely, as if she were inventing as she went along.

"This is a farm, you know," she added, more firmly.

"Why, yes," said Rayanne, "of course." She was beginning to feel she could dissemble as convincingly as the next person. She decided to investigate this sudden new confidence later. For now she added, "And we've taken enough of your time. We need to be getting back to Alexandria."

They thanked Elizabeth for the tea and saw themselves out. Elizabeth had asked them whether they minded if she didn't walk them to the door. They had been only too relieved to answer in the negative.

As they headed for Sandy and the waiting car Rayanne asked Noor in a voice that she hoped didn't carry back to the house, "She's an old woman, right?"

Noor nodded as if she actually didn't think Rayanne was crazy to ask.

"How fast do you think she can get to Ferlin's tool shed?"

"Over there by the creek?"

"Yeah."

"Not as fast as we can, if that's what you're asking."

"O.K. Let's be quick about it, then," said Rayanne. "But don't run!" Noor had seemed to pick up some urgency from Rayanne's concern and would have bolted if Rayanne hadn't caught her.

Rayanne didn't look back over her shoulder at the house but she had the distinct impression they were being watched. Oh, boy, she thought, we'll never get invited back here. Then they walked quickly, very quickly to the tool shed.

CHAPTER 46

▼

CHICKENS

The tool shed door was half open. The interior looked dark but they pushed the door open and light gushed in behind them and brightened everything. The walls were vertical planks, the floor was dirt and the gardening equipment, much of it gasoline powered, was covered with a thick reddish brown dust, caked and streaked.

But they took no time to look around. Against the far wall there was a cot, like a day bed but one that had seen lots of use. Beside the day bed was not a bucket but a jar, a Mason jar, containing what looked like blood, somewhere between the color red and the color black. But the most compelling thing in the room was the man lying on the cot. He struggled weakly to raise his head at the sight of them.

It was Ferlin. His eyes worked frantically from Noor's face to Rayanne's and back again. "Elizabeth?" he asked.

His expression, his expressions, for there were two of them, alternated between manic glee and drunken despair. His face was like a jerky home movie, jumping from one look to the next and back again.

Kneeling on the floor beside the bed was Sandy. Her face, though sweating, looked calm by comparison. "We can save him," she said looking from Noor to Rayanne. "We need a hospital, though." She looked in disgust at the jar on the floor. "He's going to need blood."

✳   ✳   ✳   ✳

Sandy was strong. Ferlin in his condition was light, even for a thin person. She carried him unassisted out to the car and propped him up against one side of the back seat. She got in beside him. No words had been spoken.

Rayanne looked at him with concern and turned to Noor. "We have to tell Elizabeth."

"You can't do that! Look at what she's done to him."

"Verajean … Noor!" What a time to make that slip. Rayanne gritted her teeth. "It's gotta be done."

"She's not going to let you take him to the hospital."

"There's three of us. She can't stop us."

"She can call the police."

"I don't think she would."

Noor looked unconvinced. Rayanne knew they were running out of time and the knowledge gave her power. "Now!"

This time they ran. All the way to the steps. They knocked but they didn't stop. They went running in. Elizabeth was not in the big kitchen. They tried the darkened rooms opening off the hallway. There were boxes and covered things in room after room, with more of the back-to-nature carvings, fetishes and decorations. Walls covered with pictures of people in old fashioned clothing. Even young people, all dressed in out-of-style wear. No sign of Elizabeth.

The backdoor was screened and unlatched. They went out, bumping each other in the door frame. There was no one visible in the yard. The closest structure was the chicken house, surrounded by a fence. The fence yard door was slightly open but no chickens had found their way to freedom.

Inside the chicken house Elizabeth's body lay stretched across the floor, one leg against the water pan. Rayanne started forward then turned away—a strong urge to throw up.

The chickens had gone for the eyes first.

CHAPTER 47

▼

EPILOGUE

"She must have loved those chickens," said Rayanne.

"She was a crone," said Noor. "She would have known what to take."

"Yeah," said Sandy. "She'd a' gone fast and painless."

"No," said Rayanne.

Lieutenant Coelho looked at her, wearing his trying-to-understand-women look.

"No, what?" he asked.

"No. Just no," said Rayanne. There was a fierce look in her eye. She showed him out the door and into the street.

She watched him walk away, running sneakers with a rumpled business suit. She thought of an unfinished painting of herself, begun in blues, still to be finished in blues.

She thought she would make just one change. She would draw one breast hung slightly lower than the other, one nipple slightly, no, *definitely* less perky.

978-0-595-43638-5
0-595-43638-2

Made in the USA
Middletown, DE
04 April 2022